YOU ARE SLOTH!

STEVE LOWE

ERASERHEAD PRESS
PORTLAND, OREGON

Also by Steve Lowe:

Muscle Memory
King of the Perverts
Samurai vs. ROBO-DICK
Mio Padre, il Tumore

YOU ARE SLOTH!

ERASERHEAD PRESS
205 NE BRYANT STREET
PORTLAND, OR 97211

WWW.ERASERHEADPRESS.COM

ISBN: 978-1-62105-101-5

Printed in the USA.

DEDICATION:

As always, this is for Michele. And for all the sloths I've loved
before.

PART ONE: POWER ANIMAL

CHAPTER ONE

The dude writes, "You are sloth!" and that's how it begins.

Bam, sloth.

He didn't write "a sloth," just sloth, and that has you wondering what he means. It concerns you a little that this is some kind of *Se7en* thing where you're going to die in a very lazy way because some foreign spammer has seen too many American movies without quite grasping their gist.

Some hairy, sweaty, unclean guy somewhere in Kazakhstan hunkered down in front of a ten-year-old computer still running Windows 95, whiling away his days pumping out millions of atrociously-worded emails and watching torture porn like it's an instructional video.

Probably the guy has directed or even starred in a few of his own. And now you're going to become a cast member. (You also assume *he* is a he because, well, why wouldn't you, right?)

But that wasn't what he meant.

When he says, "You are sloth," he's being quite literal, but in your hangover haze, that just flies right on by. You just don't get it until you reach for the keyboard to respond and instead spend ten minutes staring at your yellow, curved fingernails (three to be exact; you count them over and over to confirm) and thin paws covered in long, wiry hair.

You try to scream, and something akin comes out, but it ain't you, and it ain't natural. You try to stand up from your desk, but you can't because you're already standing. You have to jump down from your chair and scuttle down the hall to the bathroom, chuffing and chortling some choked alien cry all the way. You feel like you're running, but you're not getting anywhere too fast. You finally get to the bathroom, and you're just tall enough to see over the vanity and catch a glimpse of yourself in the bottom of the mirror.

Through the milky dots of crusted toothpaste splatters, you see and you understand.

A motherfucking sloth.

* * *

But first, how did this happen?

It starts here:

You tried to bang your landlady in exchange for rent.

Trouble was, she totally cock-blocked you.

While you haven't been with a large number of women in your life, you've at least got experience with a respectable number of young ladies, all of whom (well, most of whom) were better looking, much younger, and less hairy than Mrs. Lautrec, but she didn't seem to pick up that vibe.

The bitch of it was you'd be doing her a favor, really. It's not like she's got moderately attractive, generally nonthreatening, or, at the very least, disease-free men pounding down her door, offering her a piece of choice young ass. If there weren't a question of income hanging in the balance, you'd practically be eligible for sainthood by making such an offer.

She didn't see it that way. She held up her fist in your face and leaned in close enough that you could count the individual black hairs on her upper lip and said, "What you think I am, some harlot? Floozy?"

She's got this thick French-Canadian accent that normally would be pretty hot, if she hadn't neglected to wax her mustachio for a month, or if her breath didn't smell like hummus. You ratcheted up the charm, figured double or nothing, not like you could lose any more at that point.

"Mrs. L, no, I think you misunderstood me. I was speaking in American colloquialisms that perhaps you interpreted the wrong way."

"I live here for thirty-six years. I forget more American than you know."

She leaned in closer, close enough that the tips of her huge, low-slung cross-your-hearts were mere centimeters from contacting your upheld palms. You detected notes of red wine among the scent of mashed chickpea. You saw a glimmer of hope that maybe if you got her drinking, she'd be more pliable.

She seemed to be sizing you up, hovering there uncomfortably. Looking from one eye to the other, taking an expedition inside your head. Making you start to sweat. Finally, after her summation was complete, her assessment sure to be surprisingly accurate and entirely depressing, she sneered at you. "Maybe as younger lady I would fall for shtick, but I am not younger lady. You would not know how to satisfy mature woman with complex desires such as Widow Lautrec. Go back to your room and play on your video games, little boy."

She pinched your cheek like you were a fourth-grader who said something adorable. You stood there, stunned, and watched her saunter down the hall toward the dingy stairs, her middle-aged lady's rump swishing back and forth beneath a flower-print skirt. She paused at the top step and looked back over her shoulder, and you popped a chub, a wholly unexpected result of the psychological undressing she had just administered.

"You have one week for rent, boy," she said. Then she was gone. As soon as the echoes of her heels clomping down the metal stairs faded away and you heard the slam of her first floor apartment door, Cross joined you out in the hall.

"Damn, loser, she stepped on your sack pretty hard there, huh?"

You were not in any kind of mood to deal with Cross, but that didn't matter at all to him. Either he struggled to read social cues, or he simply didn't give a damn about them. You figured it was the latter.

"Hi, Chris," you said with a drippy smile. Cross hated that

name, which was why he went by Joe, his middle name, or simply eschewed everything in favor of his surname. But you knew this, which he hated as well. He despised his mother for slapping the name Christopher Cross on him, a double-whammy of cheese. On the playgrounds of his modest youth, he was either laughed at for being named after the loser from the '80s who sang "Sailing" or he was called Kris Kross and laughed at for being named after the little backwards-clothes-wearing shopping-mall-ghetto tools from the 90's. To be saddled with a moniker steeped in fading, flash-in-the-pan pop culture was an affront to everything Cross believed in, and probably the reason for those beliefs in the first place.

The reason you knew of his embarrassing name and upbringing was because he drunk-knocked your door one night, and for nearly an hour, you learned many wonderful, personal details about your shanty Irish, wanna-be yuppie, product-of-a-trailer-park neighbor, all of which he never would have told you had he not first downed half a bottle of Laphroaig because it made him feel sophisticated.

He bristled at hearing his birth name and straightened his coat, held his shoulders back to let the insult wave wash over him, then resumed his typical swagger.

"Money problems, then?" he said.

Everything was about money with this guy. If you didn't have it, or weren't killing yourself daily in the manic quest to acquire large piles of it so you could dive into it and swim around, Scrooge McDuck-style, then you were nothing.

"More like woman problems," you said. "If you're not sure what I'm talking about, I can explain. You see, there are times when a man feels certain urges, the need to enjoy the company of a lady, and—"

"Bitch, please." Cross smartly adjusted his tie and inflated his chest. "I suppose you didn't see the little cum receptacle I kicked out of here this morning, then."

"Nope, suppose I didn't."

"You were probably too busy cranking one off in the darkness before the warm glow of a computer screen. And speaking of the ways of the bitch, allow me to give you a little piece of advice."

You turned to face Cross and clasped your hands to your chest. "Oh, goody! I was praying you would impart a morsel of your romantical wisdom unto me."

"Eat a dick, fucktard."

"That's your advice? To eat a dick? Because this works for you?"

Cross ignored your insult and forged ahead, keen on sharing his wisdom.

"Woman problems are a myth, and easily handled."

"Really? How's that, Casanova?"

"Women are only a problem if you let them become one."

"Wow. The bullshit's coming out a bit vague these days, don't you think?"

Cross snatched up the briefcase resting next to his right leg and hefted it importantly. "No bullshit, just clear-minded thinking. Let me put it to you this way, since your retard shields are apparently set for 'dullard.' There are millions upon millions of women out there. You could literally have your pick of the litter; you just have to stop worrying about being rejected. The only thing that's keeping you from banging as many whores as you want is your fear that one of the skanks might say no. Your objective in dating up to this point has been to avoid rejection. But if your end game was simply to dip your wick, and it should be, then you need not worry about any of the typical dating game bullshit like being polite and treating her with respect and listening to her talk about a bunch of female horseshit. That's all just distraction. Sliding your hose into her cooter is the objective, nothing more. When you have yourself a clear objective, then you can go after that objective with utmost confidence. And in the end, that's exactly what a really classy bitch is looking for. She wants a classy guy, who's got confidence spurting out of his dick, and she wants that shit shot all up inside of her, even if she pretends otherwise. So if you can come at 'em like that, you'll have bitches in and out so often you won't be able to keep track without a spreadsheet. Which, by the way, isn't a bad idea, either."

You stared at him for a moment then broke into an ovation. "Bravo. That was impressive. Nothing says *classy man* like calling his classy lady a 'little cum receptacle.' Do you own some kind of offensive word thesaurus, or asshole phrase-of-the-day calendar? Perhaps a newsletter for dickheads you subscribe to?"

Cross smacked you on the shoulder as he pushed by, on his way to whatever greed-driven sociopathic endeavor he did for a living. "No problem, dipshit. I have a charitable streak in me sometimes, and I'm usually willing to help out morons who so desperately need my guidance. Hey, that's not a bad idea, either. Maybe I should start a newsletter for retards. You know, give fuckheads pointers on how to be less fuckheaded. Set it up as a 501C tax shelter or something."

"Your benevolence is most humbling."

Cross waved as he walked away, and you turned to your apartment door so you could go back inside and put into practice Mrs. Lautrec's gaming advice. Before you could get inside, Cross stopped and walked back a few steps, his familiar shit-eating grin plastered on his smug, smoothly-shaven face.

"Oh, I nearly forgot," he said. "Next time you run into Randy the Retard, ask him about Hitler."

You considered ignoring the comment altogether and forging ahead with your day, but you simply couldn't resist hearing what cruel ruse Cross was now playing on your other unfortunate third-floor neighbor. "Why am I asking him about Hitler?"

"I was making fun of his shitty little mustache the other day and I asked him if he was trying to look like Hitler. And he says to me, 'Who's Hitler?'"

"He didn't know who Hitler was?"

"No clue. So I told him to look it up and when I see him the next day, I say, 'So, Dr. Jones, what did you unearth about my man Adolf?' And he starts telling me everything he learned about Hitler and the Nahzees."

"The wha-zees?"

Cross coughed up a laugh. "He was saying Nazis, but instead of pronouncing it with that hard Notzee sound, he kept saying 'Nahzee.'"

"He's never heard the proper pronunciation of Nazi?"

"I shit you not."

"How can one go through their entire life and never once hear that word?"

Cross shrugged and held up his non-briefcase-carrying hand. "It's medically impossible, but if anyone could do it, it's Randy the Retard."

You just shook your head and walked into your apartment. Cross laughed and went on his way, his smartly buffed wingtips clonking down the stairs as noisily as Mrs. L's heels had. Before you closed your door all the way, Cross's voice echoed down the passage one last time, filling your apartment like a cloud of noxious gas.

"Have a good day, Short Bus. Try not to jack off to Lady Lautrec more than about half a dozen times, 'k buddy?"

You latched the door and stood there wondering why you bothered talking to that guy at all. Then you went and called up Mrs. Lautrec from your spank bank to make a withdrawal. You spent the rest of that day hating yourself for it, too.

CHAPTER TWO

That wasn't the point where you turned into the sloth, but we're getting there.

First, you got stiff-armed by Lady Lautrec.

Next, you got life-coached by Armen Lamont Gruber.

Gruber was your job at that moment, and the only one. Which is why the rent had come and gone past due, and you hadn't been able to pay it. Your freelance job as an editor for a tiny publishing company that puts out shitty self-help books is not what the Craigslist ad had made it out to be.

That entire website had pretty much become the bane of your existence, thanks to some ass named ArmyG403. Your own ad for freelance editing included your cell number, which ends with 6161. ArmyG403's ad, located in the "men looking for men" section, included a number which ended in 1616. It was amazing how many dyslexic homosexuals there were in this city.

As if to prove that point, the phone rang at that moment. You considered not answering it because you knew what it was, and it was nothing you wanted to think about. You looked up ArmyG403's ad and had yet to reconcile what you found there. It's not like you were a prude or grew up in an Amish community and just now had begun to discover life outside Lancaster county. You had no problem with homosexuals. Live free or die, man. The world needed more sex and love, especially your world. But this was something much stranger. The specificity of this particular advertisement for anonymous butt sex included more than simple man-on-man relations.

The exact line read: "Looking for bottom with furry friends to WATCH ONLY. The more exotic the better. Endangered species GREATLY desired."

So, animals were involved, and you weren't sure what role they played in the desired hookup. You would like to think they don't get involved in the physical portion of any rendezvous, but what happens behind closed doors, away from prying eyes? And who is watching whom? And how exactly did the inclusion of an albino Burmese python or a relict leopard frog increase one's sexual excitement? You looked it up and the closest thing you found was faunoiphilia, which is watching animals mate with each other. And there's also Zoophilia, which is an attraction to the animals themselves. But if the ad was to be believed, the beasts were there just to serve as an audience, which asked the question: what's weirder, wanting to watch animals fuck, or wanting animals to watch *you* fuck?

There were so many good reasons to ignore that incoming call, but if you didn't answer it, there was a chance you could be missing an opportunity. Someone, finally, could be in desperate need of emergency manuscript editing. The kind of emergency where people shout, "Price is not an issue! I need results, and fast!"

You needed money, and fast. You answered the phone.

It was not opportunity calling. It was someone named Dickie.

"Sorry, you have the wrong number."

The voice on the other line, this Dickie guy, didn't believe you.

"Um… So where should we meet up?"

You pushed at the migraine pushing back against your eyes.

"Dude, listen to me. You have the wrong number. This is not ArmyG403."

A beat. Another beat. Panting on the line.

"I love your cock. It's really pretty. You have a pretty cock. I sent you back a pic of mine. Did you get it?"

You wonder if the guy was talking about a penis, or an actual rooster. It was a toss up between the two, and you decided you didn't really want to know. Fucking Craigslist.

"Listen, Dickie. I am going to speak slowly. I am going to enunciate every syllable for you. I am praying you will understand this time. Are you ready?"

Beat, beat. Pant. "Yeah."

"I. Am. Not. ArmyG403."

Silence.

"You. Have. The. Wrong. Number."

Not silence, but not talking. Breathing. Was he jogging?

"What?"

"Oh, for fuck's sake."

You gave up and disconnected. Rubbed your temples and worked to forget about Dickie. A minute later, the phone rang again. Same number. Dickie still not understanding his mistake. You thumbed the ringer to zero and considered just putting it on silent, but couldn't bring yourself to do that. You thumbed it back up to two.

This was the game you played every day.

You returned to your work. Armen Lamont Gruber's manuscript was sent to you as a PDF, replete with images and cover. All you needed to do was go through the final layout one last time and spot typos. Nothing else. Your commentary on the content was not only discouraged, it was outright forbidden. Just read the words, track any corrections, of which there were many, and shoot it back in a week.

That was five days ago. You were still on page 102 of 373. You seriously wondered if anyone had read the book yet, or if the publisher simply slapped on a cover before sending it to you. It was bad enough, slogging through Gruber's strange patois of self-help-themed drivel, trying to discern what was a typo and what was intentional, but you were also behind and now had major lag. You sat there, watching the little icon spin and spin, waiting, wondering if it was frozen, or still chugging.

Should you reboot? Should you control-alt-delete? As soon as you did that, it would load and you would see it for one brief second, and then it would be gone and you would have to wait for the whole thing to start over, and then you would be right back where you are now, hovering inches from your screen, watching the little icon spin-spin-spin, wondering when (if) it would finally load up. Lag is quite the vicious cycle.

An hour later, you have half the file loaded. Good enough to get started. You're in the part of the book where Gruber is talking about power animals. To quote:

Power animal is not inspiration. Power animal is representative of your insides. Not the guts and things sloshing about in your thick belly. Your intangible persona. Your essence of who you are. Power animal is not meant to inspire you to be something you are not. Power animal is a mirror to reflect what you really are.

All have a power animal inside them. But not all animals are powerful. It is not the animal that decides this, because an animal is not smart. It is the person that decides this, because they are human. The animal provides the power and the human provides the smart. This is the way nature intended. But not all humans are smart, either. This is one of nature's practical jokes it plays on you. Humans are born with the gift of critical thinking, as compared to the instinctual animal. But not all humans are critical thinkers. Many, many humans are quite stupid. Evidence of this is found in the popularity of network television, light beer commercials, and the Internet.

'But, Armen,' you ask, 'if the peoples are stupid, how do they power animal?' To which I say - the choosing of your power animal is made by who you are, not what you wish to be. A man who wants to be lion, but is meerkat in daily life of activities and mind thoughts, will be meerkat in power animal. Very few humans are the lion with their power animal. No one is aggressive and strong enough to be king of the jungles. Few humans have the power to be king of the shopping mall food court. This is not how peoples work.

That was page 103. Only 269 pages to go. In two days.

With that, you decided to take a break. Maybe in the time

it would take to drink a beer, the rest of the book would be loaded. This was going to be a long night. Your phone buzzed, and you looked at the screen. Dickie, again.

What would Dickie think of power animals? Gruber's book might be like reading *Penthouse Forum*. He wouldn't get through two pages of it before his balls erupted.

Maybe you'd have two beers.

CHAPTER THREE

The hesitant knocking at your door told you who was on the other side. It was Randy. A walking, talking, breathing example of Armen Lamont Gruber's stupid theory.

You felt bad for Randy, so you didn't call him a retard like that asshole Cross, but it was hard not to do so. If you did, your usage of the term would not be derogatory, but clinical. It was quite likely that Randy had already been diagnosed with something, or he would be if he ever saw a doctor. The guy put the stupid in the word *stupid*.

"Hey, man. You home?"

He asked this as he stood just outside the door to your home, looking at you standing inside your home.

"Yeah, Randy. I'm home."

"Cool."

He stood there for a long beat, as though it was your turn to talk. So you said, "Did you need something? Because I'm kind of trying to work."

Randy looked down at the beer in your hand and smiled.

"Oh, okay. I was just checking to see if you were home. It's kind of boring for a Thursday."

"It's Friday, Randy."

He smiled. "Oh, really? Sweet, TGIF then!"

"Yeah, TGIF. Look, again, I have some work to do..."

At that, he came in, as though you had just invited him, rather than tried to get rid of him.

"Got any more beers?" He asked this as he stuck his head inside the refrigerator and pulled one out. You sighed.

"Yeah, help yourself. Nothing special, just some cheap shit that was on sale."

Randy held up the bottle of off-brand light lager you had bought at the discount grocery store that got all its stuff from Canada. It came in a green bottle and had a weird, German-looking name that was suspiciously close to Weimaraner, and tasted suspiciously like dog urine might if said dog urine had been bottled and refrigerated and packaged in a container that was just different enough to keep the company from being sued by Heineken or Beck or one of those real German imports. The six-pack even said *Imported* on the side, but that was technically true, since it was imported dog piss from Canada.

"Cool, this is my favorite kind."

Of course it was.

Randy plopped on the couch, and you wavered in the hallway between your sparse living room and your even-more-Spartan bedroom/home office, considering the cost of putting off nearly 300 pages of hardly readable, only partially English text so you could sit and drink beer and have withering, soul-crushing conversations with Randy.

But really, it wasn't much of a choice. You grabbed two more beers from the fridge and plopped down next to Randy. Neither of you said much as you powered through that initial beer and moved on to the next one. Couldn't let these things sit too long, lest they become anything but ice cold. That's when you really detected the notes of canine uric acid in the brew.

"Randy, have you ever heard of people wanting to have sex while their pets watched them?"

"Who's having sex with pets?"

"Actually, nevermind."

Randy was quiet a moment, then said, "I agree."

You belched and replied, "You agree with what?"

"That it's Friday."

"Yeah, that was more of a statement of fact than a matter of opinion. It's not really something with which you either agree or disagree, it's simply a matter of confirming whether or not it's true."

"You make a strong case."

"Randy, I'm not making a case. This is just basic logic."

"You writers sure have a way with words."

It was time to drop this conversation before your head exploded. Quite surprisingly, Cross bailed you out with a hard rap at the front door. For possibly the first time ever, you were glad to see him when he poked his head through and said, "Getting the homo party started a little early, eh boys?"

Randy waved and said, "Hi, Cross."

Cross shut the door behind him, and you saw the friendly shape of a whiskey bottle in his right hand. Cross patted his knee like he was beckoning a puppy and said, "Hi, Randy! How ya doin' little buddy? Did'ya have a good day, huh? Did'ya take some naps and chew on your bone, huh?"

Randy laughed and said, "Good one! You got me."

You wondered if he really had done those things. The chances were pretty high.

"What are you doing here, Cross? No classy ladies to ensnare in your web of charm on a Friday night, or did you run out of Rohypnol?"

"Hilarious, fucktard. You had all day to work on something, and that's the best you came up with? You call yourself a writer."

Cross walked into the kitchen and rooted around in your cabinets.

"Got any clean glasses in here, or am I gonna need a Hep B test tomorrow morning?"

You ignored his question, drained your beer and pointed at Cross's whiskey. "What's the special occasion?"

He joined you and Randy in the living room with the whiskey in one hand and three glasses pinched in the fingers of the other.

"Who needs a special occasion to get lit?" He set the bottle and glasses on the coffee table and went to work on the cap. "Cancel your plans, girls, because we're not leaving here until this fucker is gone."

He laughed before you could respond and said, "Man, I'm hilarious. Like you losers had any plans."

"I actually have quite a bit of work to do," you said, but your heart wasn't in it.

"Right, which is why you're sitting here drinking shitty beer with a retard. I'm guessing that's not part of your assignment."

"I was taking a break." You reached for the glass Cross handed to you.

Randy said, "How was your day? Where do you work again?"

Cross drained three fingers with a growl and poured another. "Downtown, the finance district. And my day was productive as hell, like usual. Making money just comes easy to some people. But you guys wouldn't know about that."

"If you're so successful," you said, trying like hell not to slur your words already, but not having much success, "why do you live here? Why don't you have some snazzy joint with a view of the lake and a closet full of knives and power tools to dismember women with?"

"You watch too much TV, kid," Cross said. "And nice preposition at the end of that sentence, Hemingway. To answer your poorly worded query, I live here because I'm fuckin' smart. I don't waste my money on bullshit like that because I'm sticking it all in the bank so I can retire in ten years and live the rest of my days in the lap of luxury while you two cunts are deciding how to spend your food stamps."

"Well, aren't you just a font of knowledge. We should feel honored by your mere presence, I suppose."

"I'll drink to that." Cross drained his second glass and refilled all three.

At that rate, the bottle wasn't going to last long. You fetched another beer from the fridge to chase the whiskey, lest you end up completely hammered before the sun even went down.

Cross said, "How can you possibly drink that piss?"

"I drink it because that's all I could get with my food stamps, Scrooge McDuck."

Cross stood and walked around your living room, poking at your sparse furnishings. Taking stock of your life as represented by what was laying around your apartment. He pulled a North Face jacket off the coat rack and turned up his nose.

"No wonder you don't have cash for quality liquor. You blow it on trendy bullshit."

"What, exactly, do you have against my jacket?"

"It's not the jacket; it's the logo on the back. I don't care if the parcel is any good or not. North Face is like the Honda Accord of clothing. It's the Sierra Nevada of outerwear. Sure, it's well made and decent for the price, but everybody has one now. Shit, I bet Randy's even got one."

Randy bobbed his head off his chest at the mention of his name. "Present!"

"Do you really want people to see you wearing the same brand name as this mental midget?"

Randy giggled. It was debatable whether he knew Cross was talking about him. Unlikely, based on his nodding agreement.

"It's a douche stamp, just like drinking Pabst Blue Ribbon in public or wearing knit hats in the summer. If you have to be trendy, at least get a Patagonia. Make half an effort to be a little more original, for Christ's sake!"

You were slurring your words, no matter how hard you tried to control your lips. It was a lost cause at that point, so you gave up. "Okay, Mr. Sartorial Guru, I see your point." You feigned writing with an invisible pen and pad, hoping he was picking up your sarcasm. "Keep going. I want to make sure I get all the high points down. This is important stuff."

Cross moved to your entertainment center and began to rummage through the drawer, rattling your collection of DVDs.

"Jesus Christ on a crutch." He held up your special collector's edition of *Iron Man*. "Your next step would be to grab an industrial strength trash bag and toss every one of these goddamn things in it."

"Not a fan of movies, either?"

"No, I mean these particular movies."

"What, you have a problem with super hero movies, too?"

Randy giggled again and chimed in. "Yeah, what's your problem with super movies, hero?" He sounded as drunk as you were beginning to feel. You wondered if Cross had roofied the drinks.

His face turned a deep crimson as he prepped for another monologue. "These movies have come to represent a generation-long nightmare of epic proportions." You had to hand it to the guy; he certainly seemed sincere. He stood and straightened his shoulders, launching into full-on rant mode.

"The man of today is little more than a comic-book-movie-watching, gay-trend-following, pud-pounding ponce, lacking a single shred of self respect. Fat, slobby, perpetuating the TV-sitcom myth that men must be overweight and stupid, lest they be considered sexist, racist, materialistic homophobes who cause all the world's problems and are deserving of all the world's white-hot hatred. Every Cheeto-gorging, lite-beer-swilling, Internet-porn-sneaking, sweaty-fisted prole who rushes out to see these pieces of shit is only reinforcing that stereotype to the point that it becomes fact rather than media manufactured exaggeration. Men shouldn't be going to movies in general. They should be chasing wool. The only reason to sully one's feet on the tacky floor of a movie theater is if it helps to accomplish that singular goal."

You sat there with Randy, staring slack-jawed at Cross, whose chest heaved from the exertion. It was a full 30 seconds before you began a slow golf clap, which Randy joined until the two of you were standing, clapping wildly.

"That," you said, "was incredible."

Randy leaned sideways and stumbled into you. "Yeah!"

"The pure belief you have in your own bullshit is simply astounding."

Cross grinned and threw back his whiskey. He nearly fell over while reaching for the bottle to re-fill his glass. You leaned over for your own and felt the hot blood rush of drunkenness fill your face. Holding down the contents of your stomach was a supreme chore, on which you focused all of your attention, vaguely hearing Randy and Cross discuss the finer points of a number of topics you did not, and would not, recall.

At some point, you realized the sun had gone down, and congratulated yourself on not passing out completely before then. A moment of clarity in your memory dragged up an image of Randy in his underwear, the front of his shirt soaked through, and Cross, his tie around his forehead and a lighter in his hand, holding the flame up to Randy's shirt and laughing so hard that no sound came from his open-mouthed, beet-red face.

That image recedes into your fuzzy mind. You recall no more from the evening. You are left with nothing but your own altered visage staring back from the bathroom mirror, all dark fur covering a round head, and what looks like a permanently frozen smile on your slothy face that does not accurately reflect your current level of pants-shitting panic.

CHAPTER FOUR

You clamber up onto your chair and stand with your fuzzy sloth chest resting against the paint-chipped desk. It was an old thing you salvaged from a curbside junk pile a few months back when you moved into this apartment. The same week, both Cross and Randy had moved into the building as well, and the desk had been a leftover relic from one of their places, chucked out for the garbage in favor of something new and clean and not covered in some stranger's foreign bodies.

It bore old, suspicious stains, and gave you splinters in the heels of your hands at first, until the wood and paint wore smooth from use, but it was what you could afford, which was to say, nothing.

The faded scent of stale smoke had cured into the gray wood over the years, but it suddenly seems more potent. As are distinct notes of ass and sweat and some combination of the two, drifting up to your newly sensitive sloth nostrils. Did you really smell this bad? Was it noticeable to others? Why the hell do you give a shit about it right now? You're a fucking sloth. Shouldn't you be worrying about *that* rather than whose olfactory sensibilities you might offend?

Yes, you most definitely should.

You track back again to the night before, but no new memories surface from the fog of good Irish whiskey and bad beer chasers. No recollection of how you ended up in this chair, how long you sat there, passed-out-blinding drunk or damn near so, at what point you decided it was a good idea to check your email, or open something from the Phillipino

Sherrif's Attache to East Berlin, or for that matter, actually click any fucking links included therein.

You never do boneheaded shit like that. You're paranoid enough to know that every email that hits your inbox has the potential to infect your computer. You don't forward, you don't share, and you sure as shitfire don't open attachments or click on hinky-looking links that end in .*de*.

But last night, you did it anyway. In a haze of alcohol from which you have yet to fully emerge, you opened that email marked SPAM:HIGH, with the all caps subject line, YOU ARE SLOTH.

Now what the fuck should you do?

Is this some new kind of virus, one that doesn't infect your computer, but rather infects your actual, physical being? Is this a government hacking thing, a new form of modern warfare, perhaps accidentally released on an unsuspecting public? Stuxenet 2.0, now with more sloth? Are you part of a top-secret experiment gone horribly wrong? Or, fucking hell, gone horribly right? Are you St. George, Utah, but rather than nuclear testing fallout, you're a different kind of guinea pig casualty?

How will you explain this to people? Can you even do that? You're a sloth now. Can you even talk anymore? Or will you spend the rest of your misspent life squeaking out some freaky sloth garble and be sent to a zoo where the other sloths will sniff you out for the fake you are and beat your ass daily like it's the lockup in Joliet? Is there such a thing as sloth rape? Are zoo sloths just like convicts? Will they open your ass like a jar of pickles, regardless of their sloth sexual orientation?

You don't want to go to animal jail. You really, really don't want that.

And come to think of it, what is your sexual orientation, anyway? Are you a boy sloth? You bend forward, craning your sloth neck to check out your sloth goods. You whack your sloth head against your scrap-pile desk and wobble, tottering on unstable sloth legs until you tumble backwards into the chair. Thankfully, it's large enough for you to lie back without falling off, and you take a minute to clear your mind. But that's just not happening right now. Calm is not descending, because you need answers to some of these questions.

You reach a horrifying, curved monster claw between your legs and gently root around, not sure what you'll find. After a thorough examination, with much care taken so as not to lop off anything with your Edward Scissorhands, you discover multiple protrusions amid the fur there which feel quite a bit like you do indeed have yourself a set of male sloth junk. Not very large male sloth junk, but maybe sloths don't pack much heat in general. That's what you tell yourself. You really don't care, though. You're just happy you've got something downstairs.

"Thank fucking Christ!"

You jump at the sound of your voice. Mostly because it's your voice.

"Holy hairy pants pissers!"

Your mouth is moving, your throat is vibrating, your tongue is contacting the roof of your sloth mouth. You are definitely the one providing the sound effects here. And you sound very much like the real you.

"SHIT COCK BALLS ASS PUSSY CUNT VAGINA TITS!"

Your mind is clear of all else but this. You go with it.

"ASS FUCKINGLY BITCH RAPING!"

Okay, that's good. The grammar sucks, but you feel a little bit better. Something at least is still the same. You check your package again and decide it, too, is proportionally the same, which is pretty goddamn depressing. If you're going to be turned into an animal, you could at least be done the favor of becoming something that's a little more hung and virile than a FUCKING SLOTH.

"Thanks, Jesus. That's real fucking fair. Couldn't be a horse, huh? Had to be a sloth."

You sit there, mindlessly rubbing your nubs with one paw

and staring at the other, splaying out all three claws, sniffing and licking.

"Just getting the lay of the land here, Jesus. Since you saw fit to turn me into the one animal I know fuckall about."

You stand and wiggle your claws over the computer keyboard. You need information. You need to know more. You need Wikipedia.

After several minutes of fumbling over the keys and typing nothing close to the English language thanks to your shishkabob skewer claws, you finally get a hunt-and-peck system down and do some info gathering. You are not a marsupial as you originally suspected. You're just a goddamn sloth. You're a slow-moving, ass-picking, waste of evolutionary space. You're the dipshit of the jungle.

You learn that your hair is home to something called symbiotic cyanobacteria, which live on you and fuck on you and shit and piss on you and make millions of tiny new cyanobacteria while you spend your days hanging in trees, eating leaves and picking dingleberries off your ass with your toilet claws.

"Fuck you, I hate salads! Why the hell can't I be a carnivore? Ass face!"

You find your way to YouTube and watch video after mocking video. No, you're not a marsupial at all. You're a meme. You get off the Internet because it's entirely too depressing. You go back to that email and stare at the purple, clicked-on, life-ruining link. You still need answers. Real, explanatory type answers, and you've gotten nowhere. You wrestle with the mouse until you finally gain control and click Reply.

Dear Spammer Fuchead,

What the fuck is this/? What's the fuck is wrong with you? What the dfuck have you done to me? Wh7yu the fuck am I a slot?

Sincerly,

motherfucing sloth

You click Send and stare at the computer screen. What the

hell are you going to do now? Your mind is both racing and blank at the same time. You thought sloths were supposed to be slow, but your brain is chugging at warp speed and getting nowhere. Maybe *that's* why sloths are so slow. They've got some super-charged ADD that keeps them from getting anything accomplished. Their minds are a hive of counterintuitive activity that just-

Your computer dings. A new email pops up, the subject line reading: *re: (SPAM HIGH) YOU ARE SLOTH*

You click on it and read the response:

Why you are sloth? Because fuck you is why! HAHAHAHAHAHAHAHA!!!!!!!!!!!!!!!1!!

And there you have it.

* * *

You sit in your stained recliner, the only other piece of furniture in your tiny living quarters besides your couch, bed and desk. You managed to get as far as turning the TV on, but only consider the effort required to master the remote with your claws. You don't think you could handle the depression of trying and failing to work those tiny buttons. Or the physics involved in manipulating a beer cap. At least if you had cans, you could poke a hole in the side and shotgun the fucker. But no, you don't have that kind of luck.

"Saw to that too, huh, Jesus? Well done, ya prick!"

The TV had been left on some local station. You recall the last thing you watched had been *Dancing with the Stars*, and that simply deepens your gloom. The news is on, and you realize that it's already noon. Half the day is gone, but you've done little else than write an email and have a shit fit. The male and female anchors drone on and on about a sudden rash of missing persons cases. They speculate about potential hate crimes. You know all about hate crimes. Imagine the hate required to turn a human into a sloth. You drown out the insipid anchors, not at all interested in what's happening to the disappearing homosexuals of the city. You've got bigger problems.

You sit and you stare. You draw conclusions. You perform leaps of logic. Even without actual confirmation, you convince yourself of certain things. It's like some kind of sloth intuition. You know in your sloth bones it's true.

This is no government conspiracy.

You are not the subject of a top-secret cyber weapons program in the hands of rogue agents.

That would be too convenient, and actually, kind of cool.

But you don't get cool. You get mocked in an email.

You're a joke to a professional spammer with terrible grammar, just as you had feared. Some asshole in Bulgaria is sitting in front of his computer, doubled over with laughter, chortling so hard he's knocked over his bottle of oily vodka. It's splashing across the packed-dirt floor of his underground hovel in a dark, widening puddle that looks alarmingly like blood from a slashed throat, which you have no doubt he's witnessed before as well. You've seen *Hostel*. You know that shit's for real.

Somewhere nearby your phone rings. You consider making the effort to find it, but to what end? How could you possibly work the damn thing with these godforsaken shish kabobs skewers for hands? It's probably just another wrong number, some poor, confused, horny man who apparently, if local news media is to be trusted, and it's typically not, will soon turn up missing, anyway.

The phone finally stops jangling and that's when you notice a new sound, which you immediately recognize to be the incessant, annoying, doorjamb rattle of your privacy-invading neighbor, Chris Cross.

"Hey, fucko, you home?"

He pokes his head inside and looks around.

"You better not be jerking off with a cucumber up your ass," he says. "I'm counting to five and coming in. You've been given fair warning to clean yourself up and remove whatever convenient dildo apparatus you found laying around from your anus. Onetwofive."

He walks in and strides directly to the kitchen. The fridge door creaks open and crashes against the countertop. Bottles rattle and glass threatens to shatter. The fridge door slams shut, and you hear the crisp snap of a top twisting off a bottle. Sloth drool runs freely down your hairy frontside.

Silence for a moment, save for the glug of beer draining down his neck. "Aw, fuck me. This shit is so awful." Another pause, longer this time. He exhales. "Piss beer or not, I needed that. But I'm telling you right now, you need to step up a class or two in your hops and barley if you want to keep what few friends you've got."

Cross is suddenly there, right next to your chair, staring down at you, his hands frozen in the act of twisting open a second Weimaraner.

"What the fuck is this?"

You could answer him, but have no idea what to say. *Hey there, I'm a sloth now. Mind closing the door behind you?* doesn't seem to cover what all needs to be said.

"Hey, shut-in, where'd you get the Down Syndrome cat? You'd think the humane shelter would just put these disgusting things out of their misery. Fuck all that animal rights shit. You know, that's something I never understood about the tree hugging hippies. They're all for saving every sorry mistake God made when he created the world, but they sure as shit love to kill them some human fetuses."

Cross seems like he's got something else to say, but he stops and stares again. You can see him working it out. He suspects this shit ain't kosher. He's smart enough to know you're not a malformed cat. He's liable to flip that bottle over and start bashing your head in as soon as it finally hits him. You really, really have to do something. Right now.

You point at the beer and say, "Hey, dude. Can you grab me one, too?"

CHAPTER FIVE

Your first post-sloth beer is amazing. It's a symphony of delicious flavor on your sloth tongue, which after one beer has made numerous appearances outside your head, dancing around to the delight of Cross and yourself.

"Damn, kid, are you shitfaced already?"

"No, of course not," you say. But it's not true. That one beer is really hitting you fast. You attribute it to your lower body weight and the fact that your sloth plumbing hasn't been properly introduced to alcohol yet. It was going to be merely a matter of pacing yourself from now on. Just take drinks a bit slower. That certainly shouldn't be a problem for a sloth.

"I can't tell if you sound drunk, or if that's just your innate slothiness."

"I don't feel like anything is moving slower." You stand in your easy chair and gingerly lower yourself to the floor to test your coordination.

"Well, it must be relative to your own perception, because you sure as shit are moving like a sloth."

You stop touching your claws to your large nose and look at Cross, work hard to focus your doubled vision on the spot between his eyes. "I am?"

"Yeah, you are. Not that you were cheetah-like in your human form, but this is goddamn excruciating. We need to cut out the liquor and get you an upper or something. You got any crystal in this place?"

"What? No! Of course I don't have any methamphetamine! Jesus, do you think I'm some kind of junkie?"

Cross holds up his hands in mock defense. "Hey, easy, Animal Kingdom. I don't judge, you know. What you do in your spare time is not my business."

"Ha! The fuck you don't judge. The only thing I've ever heard you do is judge every single person you come into contact with, other than yourself, of course."

He empties his bottle and chucks it into the trashcan with a loud crash. "You're out of beer, dude."

"Well, thanks." You cross your arms over your hairy chest and tap a curved, yellow claw to what passes for your chin. "I had the one, which means, you had the other eight."

"I did you a favor drinking that crap. You really shouldn't be ingesting such toxins in your current state."

"Thanks for caring, Dad, but I'm not fucking pregnant. I'm a beast. And I can handle a few beers, no matter what condition my condition is in."

Cross squints at you, suddenly scheming hard at something. Whatever it is, you don't like it as a matter of principle. It's certain to be engineered for his gain alone, even if it's at your expense. *Especially* if it's at your expense. You decide to fire a preemptive strike.

"The answer is no."

"You don't even know what I was going to say."

"Doesn't matter. No."

"Just hang on a second."

"No."

"Have you looked at yourself yet?"

"Um, gee, no I haven't. Never even occurred to me to look in the mirror. Why?"

"Why?" Cross bends down and grips you under the arms, hefts you up onto his hip like a toddler. The two of you stand in front of the bathroom mirror and stare.

"What do you see?"

"Richard Grieco starring in a terrible, straight-to-DVD remake of *Every Which Way but Loose*?"

"Ha ha. That was actually pretty good. Try again, though."

"This isn't going to be some you-and-me-we're-not-so-different kind of motivational thing, is it? Because I'm really not in the mood for a pep talk."

"No, look at us. The two of us together? We're fucking adorable!"

"What are you saying?"

"I'm saying, the two of us, working as a team. Think of the wool we can tackle together. It boggles the mind."

"The what?"

"I've got the GQ thing going on over here, and you've got a hammerlock on the cute vibe."

"You've gone batshit insane."

"Hear me out. You're the perfect wingman. You've got the sweet and cuddly thing working for you, but in a handicapped sort of way. You're slow and completely non-threatening, like a stuffed animal come to life, which is totally disarming to chicks. And when they're all lubed up from playing with the cute, retarded little doggy, I'm there to reap the rewards!"

"You want me to go out with you to bars so you can use me to get laid."

"I think you sell the idea a little short when you frame it that way."

"Put me down."

"Hear me out, man. Just stop and consider it for a second."

"Put me down, or I will spray sloth shit all over the front of your sharp little Brooks Brothers ensemble, and I'm not kidding because I still haven't gone today and I have a feeling it's going to be like hot lava down the side of Krakatoa by the time I finally erupt."

Cross drops you and steps back. You take more than a little satisfaction at seeing him squirm. But he doesn't leave. He's not giving up that easy.

"I'm trying to think about your wellbeing. We need to get you out of this apartment. Fresh air will do you good. Groove to a little music; talk to some goddamn women. Grasp this opportunity. Carpe fucking diem, little sloth man."

Despite all your initial intuition that anything involving Cross equals a colossally bad idea, he's beginning to win you over. You really could stand to get out of your house for a while. Look where your hermit lifestyle had gotten you, anyway. Alone, broke, depressed, and slothy.

Cross is like a car salesman. He can sense a shift in the air. He knows he's wearing you down and he moves in for the kill.

"Come on, slothinator. Let's go introduce you to some fine bitches."

You can't believe what comes out of your slothy head next.

"Fuck it. Let's go."

Your guts rumble in response. Cross's smile fades a bit and he heads for the door. "When you're ready, then."

"Yeah, give me a few minutes here."

Maybe more than a few.

* * *

The sun has gone down by the time you emerge from the bathroom. That wasn't the midday news you were watching earlier; that was the evening newscast. The entire day has melted away and you've managed to do all of four things, one of which is a simple, basic bodily function.

Although there was nothing simple about what just happened in that bathroom. A human toilet is not exactly ideal for a sloth ass, and the only way it eventually worked out was to lower your backside through the opening and hold onto the seat edge for dear life. You close the door and leave the fan running, hopeful that the stench will dissipate over time.

Cross returns, refreshed and wearing what must be his clubbing attire. His colored shirt with jagged vertical lightning bolt stripes is painful to look at for longer than a few seconds. It's like watching a 3-D film without the special glasses.

"You can't wear that shirt. I think it's giving me a migraine."

"This atrocious shirt is a tactical choice. In regular light, it's an abomination, but in the dim, pulsing illumination of a club, this shirt attracts bitches like moths to a porch light."

"If you say so, but you really should put on a jacket or something. Distracted driving is the number one cause of accidents, you know."

Cross rubs his hands together. He's practically bouncing from foot to foot. "You ready?"

You look down at your fur. You'd tried to run a brush through it, but the wiry shit is difficult to do much with except snag. It must have some advantage out in the wild, but it definitely wasn't easy to wipe clean with toilet paper. "What about me? Should I, like, wear something, or something?"

Cross considers it for a moment. "What would be more conspicuous? A sloth, or a sloth wearing a bad shirt and hair gel?"

"Good point. I think the sloth part will be weird enough. I'm beginning to lose confidence in your assertion that I will be the chick attraction you expect."

Cross scoops you up onto his hip and you're out the door and heading for the stairs. "Shit, between you and my shirt, we'll be irresistible. In Cross we trust, little sloth man."

Trust is the last thing you're feeling at this point.

* * *

You take a cab to the club. A surprisingly responsible choice by Cross, not wanting to drive home smashed. You figured he'd want to show off some hotshot sports car, never one to miss the opportunity to let you know he was better than you and everyone else.

But he's a man on a mission. "Time to put the game face on," he says.

He pays the taxi driver and swings you up onto his hip.

"So, what should I do here?"

"Leave it to me," he says. "You might freak the chicks out if you start babbling on about something, so don't talk. Just sloth."

Like you have a choice in the matter. Cross saunters past the line of people waiting to get into the club. They're all dressed in bright colors, and some of them appear to be holding things. Are those stuffed animals? One guy is dressed as a sparkling unicorn. All of them look harshly at the two of you. There's jealousy in their eyes. Why didn't they think to bring a sloth to the club? Is this the new thing? Animal wingmen?

And it actually works. The bouncer at the door says, "The fuck is that thing?"

Cross pulls out a fifty folded in half and tucks it into the bouncer's front shirt pocket. "That is my friend, President Grant, and this is my other friend, sloth. We'll be going in together."

The bouncer, as if entranced by Cross's charm and your slothness, steps aside, and even pulls the door open for you. The crowd waiting behind the barrier watches, mesmerized. The unicorn guy groans a little bit.

The club is dark and loud, a heavy bass track slamming your chest and pulsing your eardrums from the inside out. On top of the bass is a stuttering synthesized noise that sounds nothing like the music they played in the clubs when you used to go on a regular basis. And the people writhing about inside this place look nothing like what you remember, either. Sweaty bodies wrapped in swatches of neon and tight pants and glow sticks shaped like animal ears pulse across the dance floor.

Even Cross seems to be taken aback by what he sees. No one is wearing the vertical stripes of his rapey, more youthful days. Has it been that long since you've been out to a club? Have things changed that fast? Shit, are you getting... old?

"Hey!"

Cross jumps, and you jump because he jumps. The 'hey' came from a tall, narrow girl dressed much more modestly than the sea of color out on the floor. Her dark hair is pulled back from her face, which is only half illuminated by the lighting from the dance floor, alternating shades of blue and pink and green and red, like she's a living mood ring with bipolar disorder.

"Hey," Cross says back. You have to admit, he's smooth. You need a drink before the pulsing lights and chattering dubstep set off a seizure.

"You don't look like you belong here!"

Cross gives the girl a hard up-and-down and says, "Neither do you!"

"You're right! We hadn't been for a while and decided to check it out since the new ownership took over. This place is really different now."

The song ends, and the crowd on the floor whoops and cheers. Inflatable animals are tossed into the air.

"Is this one of those rave things?"

The girl shakes her head. "I don't know what the hell this is anymore. We've been here an hour and I've managed to have four drinks and segregate the crowd into clusters."

Cross leans in closer and says, "Well, how about we make it five drinks, and you enlighten us?"

"Us?" She looks at you. "Is that thing real?"

You slowly lift a paw and wave at her. She claps her hands to her mouth and jumps. You think you've scared the shit out of her, but then she reaches out for you, a huge smile on her face.

"OH MY GOD, IT'S REAL! I LOVE MONKEYS!"

Cross tries to correct her, but she hears nothing as she pets the fur on your head. She grips you under your arms and tugs.

"Can I hold him?" Too late. She already is. She turns and heads for a dark back corner. "BECKY, LOOK AT THE MONKEY!" There's a squeal from the shadows, and then the music pumps back up and the place begins to vibrate like the inside of a heart.

You wonder where Cross is. He's been gone for some time, and the girls, Becky and Sarah, have been fawning over you, petting and prodding and laughing as they talk about a half million different subjects in a rapid-fire staccato over your head. You can't decipher any of it amid the untz-untz-untz and just sit back and relax. Looks like Cross was right. A night out of the apartment is doing you some good. Within minutes of walking into this place, you're sandwiched between two girls who are most likely attractive, though it's so dark you still haven't actually gotten a full look at either one. At least they smell nice, and they can't stop stroking you, which feels quite fine. The bumping music is beginning to rock you to sleep.

"Let's kick this party up a notch!" You snap awake, and Cross is standing there with a tray of shots, a good dozen of them in varying colors and viscosities. The girls let out a "Woo!" and reach for a glass.

"So, on my way to the bar," Cross says as he quickly passes each girl a second shot, "I think I picked up on what you were talking about. The whole crowd thing. Over to the left are a pack of dudes wearing sparkly pony shit and acting like a gang of queers."

Sarah hisses against the heat of the liquor. "Those are Bronies. They love *My Little Pony*. They're weird fuckers. Them and the Scare Bears. This place looks like a Mecca for grown-up fans of old kid shows. Over there," she points to the right where a clutch of girls wiggles around in homemade-looking outfits of painted cardboard, "are the GoBroads."

Cross shrugs, clueless.

"They're *GoBots* fangirls."

You squint through the sweaty haze and pick out a cardboard Leader-1 with boobs. You almost say something, but catch yourself in time. Instead, while the girls are distracted, Cross sitting between them now with you on his lap, you snatch a shot off the tray and toss it back.

You're instantly drunk.

Becky points to the weirdos harassing the GoBot girls. "Who're they supposed to be?"

Sarah says, "Captain Planeteers. Those guys are total assholes. No one likes them."

Cross nudges you. "I was just talking about this shit last night. This is exactly the kind of fucked up nonsense that comes from the Super Hero Movie Nerd culture. Adults dressing up like Voltron in public at a dance club. This used to be a respectable place where people looked fine and smelled great and talked about real shit like clothing and protein shakes and good whiskey, and tried like hell to get laid all night. Now it's been overrun by adult-sized children with spectrum disorders and personalities they've adopted from TV shows."

You toss down another shot and you're drunker than before. In some tiny recess of your brain, a voice of reason is screaming at you that this is all a bad idea. But you don't hear what that voice is saying because you're standing on Cross's knees, facing the three of them, trying to point at the middle person with a badly wobbling claw.

"Don't start talking shit about Voltron, asshole. That's where I draw the line."

You stumble forward and end up between Becky's breasts. It's very nice there. Warm and pleasant-smelling. The girls are squealing again. You realize they're freaking out that you spoke. Shit, you just screwed up. You weren't supposed to talk. Cross is probably pissed now. But fuck that guy. He can't just disparage Voltron and not expect a verbal smackdown. That guy is such a dick. You don't want to be here with him anym—

Cross's face in your face. You feel like you're flying. He's swinging you through the club. You technically *are* flying.

"Nice work, slothy."

Yep. He's definitely pissed. Good, because—

"Can I carry him?"

You swing through the air again. The neon colors inside the club drag across your vision like contrails. You look up and concentrate on Becky's face. She's smiling and appears to be almost as drunk as you feel. She staggers a bit and laughs so loud it stabs through your eardrums and strikes the base of your brain. You black out for a second and wake up between her breasts again. Ah, that's much better. They're the perfect size, and you snuggle your head right in there. One of them pops free from her bra. Suddenly, there's a nipple pressing against your sloth nose. You're not sure if she realizes it. There's a lot of laughter and confused conversation swirling around your head, but none of that penetrates your concentration right now because, holy shit, that's a beautiful nipple right there in your face. You can't tell if it's a right nipple or a left nipple, but what does that matter? A nipple in your face is never a bad thing.

When you come to again, you're no longer nestled between boobs. You're suddenly sad at the disappearance of Becky's nipple and you're confused for a second. You're looking down at what you slowly realize is the carpet in your apartment.

Laughter around you. Female voices. Cross saying, "Who wants whiskey?"

The girls both do. You're not sure if that's such a good idea. But what the hell. You've already made a series of questionable decisions tonight. Why not keep the streak alive?

Cross walks into the living room with an ice-filled glass and gestures to you with it. "What do you say? Feeling better? Up for a little drink?"

You look from the whiskey in his hand to the ladies at your side. The practical part of your brain is screaming about what a bad idea this is, but that's a small, distant, shrinking part. Why the hell shouldn't you? You're a goddamn sloth. What else is there to do now but get blinding drunk and make a few more poor decisions?

"What the fuck," you slur. "Start pouring."

Time ceases to be linear. You fade in and out. You feel like a year has passed when you open your eyes again.

Cross and the girls are pointing and laughing at you.

"What's so fun... What's funny? Did I fart?" All around on

the floor are remnants of a meal. That month-old package of bologna from the fridge is empty between your feet. A can of cheez whiz nearby. A pickle jar. You have a funky aftertaste in your mouth. Somewhere, faraway, you hear a dog bark.

notdognotdognotdog

"Who said that?"

Becky wobbles and falls to her knees next to you, laughing so hard she can't breathe. She finally finds enough air to say, "You're so cute I can't stand it! Where did you find such an amazing monkey?"

Cross pours whiskey into a glass and hands it to Sarah.

"He's hilarious, but that's not his only talent, ladies." Cross pours three fingers of whiskey and hands you the glass. You think you already have a glass, but that seems like days ago. "Go on, show them the tongue."

You smile, lean over your glass and nearly fall in it. You slowly extend your tongue down, down, down into the liquid and scoop out a mouthful. It's wonderful and warm at first, but slides down your sloth throat like fire and burns your belly, and you lap up more until half the glass is gone. Then you look up at the girls and swipe your tongue across your forehead.

Becky leans in close and loses her balance, falling sideways into her friend, who bowling pins into Cross, giggling and sloshing her drink on the floor.

"Oh... my goodness," Becky says.

Cross scoops Sarah from the floor and guides her toward the door. "I'm going to show Amanda here my place. You kids have fun together."

Sarah slurs, "I'm not a panda. I'm a Sarah."

"Of course you are, honey." Cross guides the stumbling girl across the hall. He leans back and pulls your door shut. "Don't do anything I wouldn't approve of."

Becky leans back on her elbows, legs splayed apart, giving you a full view of everything she's not wearing beneath her skimpy club dress. Her eyes roll back as her head lolls on her shoulders. You're not sure if she's about to pass out or if she's trying to be sexy, but it's having an effect, either way. You take another slurp from your glass and immediately feel it, such a lovely, balmy buzz all the way down to your long, yellow claws.

"That thingy in your face is really... wow," she says to the ceiling, sounding more drunk than Not-a-Panda-a-Sarah had.

You step toward her and fall flat on your little face. The room spins as you right yourself. Your crotch is wet and you realize you've spilled your drink on the way down. No matter, you plant your face in the dark stain on the carpet and slurp out the sweet nectar, never minding the fact that you haven't swept that carpet in months.

Becky's elbows give out and she flops back, her head bouncing against the floor. You don't really register this occurrence as you stagger between her legs. The scent of her womanhood attacks you, ropes you in like Wonder Woman's golden lariat. You say, "Holy shizzzz, I'm so drizzzz."

She laughs and sings, "I'm gonna get you drunk, on my hump, my hump, my hump. My lovely lady lumps." She sits up and reaches blindly with one hand until she finds your head and pulls you in. "Mix your milk with my cocoa puffs."

Then she drops flat on her back again. The last thing you remember is disappearing into a dark, warm, moist cavern from which you're not sure you'll ever return, or will ever want to, for that matter.

CHAPTER SIX

You awaken like the rising of the dead, stiff-limbed and smelling of decay.

All around you is unequivocal evidence that a sloth's digestive system should never be introduced to month-old bologna, cheez whiz and whiskey. Most likely none of those things singularly, and absolutely not in any combination.

You climb onto your recliner for a better vantage point from which to survey the damage. The carpet is a complete loss. Not that it was in good shape to begin with, but it was Taj Mahal-worthy before, compared to its current state. The only thing that could clean it now is accelerant and flame. You climb higher on the chair back to get a better view of the shape on the carpet, and can clearly see the outline of a prone girl's body amid the fecal spray.

Oh, that poor, poor creature. Becky was her name. What have you done to poor Becky? You clamber down and scuttle through the apartment, but she's not there. Probably gone screaming from the place not long before you woke up. Brown footprints leading to the door mark her escape.

You've had whiskey hangovers before, but this is something more. This is insidious. You remember almost nothing from the night before, like you'd been drugged by the CIA and dumped there. You rub your face with your paws and can still smell the sex matted into your fur. You wonder if it really happened, if you actually violated that young lady with your teeny little sloth parts. Remnants of memory slowly return. You recall descending between her thighs, and you're pretty sure that you still taste her among the other morning-breath coated flavors crusted over your tongue.

You need a bath. You need mouthwash. You need to destroy this carpet like it's evidence from a crime scene. And depending on certain laws in this state, it very likely is. You consider grabbing a beer, but you remember both what it does to you and that you are out, thanks to Cross.

Fucking Cross. That asshole. You told him you didn't want to be a part of this. You knew you shouldn't have had more to drink. You know it's not right for a beast to lie with a woman.

"Look what you created, Jesus," you croak up at the ceiling. "I'm an abomination."

In response, there's a knock at your door. You freeze and listen and know right away it's not Cross, because his rude ass simply barges in whenever he feels like it. You're curious right up to the point the key fits into the slot and the knob begins to turn. Unless Cross made copies at some point, the only person who would have a key to your apartment besides you would be Mrs. Lautrec. In other words, the last person you want to see at this moment.

As the door slowly swings open, you hurry as fast as your slow sloth limbs will carry you, into the bathroom. You peek around the corner, but she doesn't appear to have seen you. She stands just inside the door, staring straight ahead, her arms hanging at her sides.

"Hello?"

You look around the bathroom, but there's nowhere to go. You're trapped in here, and when she finds you, she's going to have herself a hissy fit. Animals aren't allowed in the building, and here you are, and out there is a massive explosion of your feces. She has to smell it.

You chance another look. Mrs. Lautrec is shuffling through the living room, past the recliner, and—holy hell. She's in her stocking feet, walking right through your mess. She doesn't see it at all, just fixes her gaze on the wall above your head.

"Hello?" she says again, but there's something strange about her voice. Monotone. Lacking that sexy, husky, French-

Canadian accent you dig so much. And, again, she's traipsing right through loose sloth dung and paying it no mind whatsoever.

She's heading for the bathroom, and you scurry back in the corner. Your only cover is a pile of musty towels, so you dive in. Mrs. L stands in the doorway for a second, seemingly not seeing you there, glassy-eyed and unfocused, then heads back the way she came. You hear her panty-hosed feet squishing across the carpet once more and battle a gag reflex, not that there could possibly be anything left inside your body to evacuate. Something is seriously fucked here.

You wait to hear the front door again, but the sound never comes. What the hell is she doing out there? Why has she come in the first place? Is she high? You never took her for a tweaker, but what do you really know about French Canadians? About as much as sloths, which is not a goddamn thing past a sketchy intestinal tract that doesn't play nice with people food.

You scoot back to the door and peer around the corner. At first you don't see her, but nope, there she is - on the couch now. She's sitting, staring across the way at the kitchen area. Not moving at all, save for the rise and fall of her breasts, which you can't help but notice are just as impressive in profile as they are head on. She sits there, doing nothing, and just when you're about to decide on a course of action, she brings her hands up from her sides and places them on that ample bosom. A moment of pause, then she begins to knead, slow at first but gradually becoming more aggressive. Her right hand remains up top, but her left hand has begun the slow descent southward. She reaches between her legs and draws her floral print skirt up to her waist.

You don't even realize you're moving until you've covered half the distance to the couch. You sidestep the nasty carpet and creep behind the recliner, knowing you should take better care not to be seen, but you're too mesmerized by the vision of a bonafide mature hottie rubbing one out on your couch. You can't believe this is happening. Had she done this before when you left the apartment? Has Mrs. L always been such a naughty little minx? Your mind reels with the possibilities.

You move to the couch as if caught in the tractor beam of this fantasy sexcapade, one of your favorite go-to scenarios actually playing out in real life before your slothy eyes. But something's not right here. Mrs. Lautrec continues to stare straight ahead, no emotion at all on her slack face. If she's enjoying herself, she's certainly not showing it. You slip out from behind the chair, into full view. The sight of a sloth sneaking up on you while you're making little circles should, at the very least, give you pause, if not completely terrify you.

But nothing happens. Her eyes remain locked on the refrigerator behind you; her left hand remains locked down betwixt her thighs; her right hand continues its rote breast groping. She looks a bit like a puppet being controlled by a horny teenaged boy who knows little about what women really do when they masturbate. You've seen enough porn to know that it never happens that way, even if this is your own first-hand experience in the presence of a self-pleasuring woman.

"Mrs. Lautrec?"

No response. She just continues to wax on and wax off.

You bang your claws together, as close to a clap as you can manage.

"Yo, Mrs. L!"

Nothing.

You scoot closer. Put a paw on her calf and give her leg a squeeze. Climb up onto the couch beside her. Try like hell not to be distracted by the rub-rub-rubbing, which takes nearly everything you can muster. You grab her shoulder and give it a shake.

"Mrs. Lautrec! Can you hear me? Hey, wake up old lady!"

Before long, you're straddling her thighs, with both paws on her shoulders, shaking her as hard as you can, but she keeps going. At the rate she's shining that thing up, tendrils of smoke should be rising from her crotch. You're sufficiently weirded out now, and you can only think of one other thing to try. You rear back and slap her across the face. It doesn't do much, though, and you smack her again, harder.

Geez, come on lady. Wake the fuck up.

Your sloth reflexes won't be able to muster much more than that, but you're about to give her one more shot when she suddenly blinks and draws in a deep breath.

Her eyes flick over you, up and down. She's finally awake from whatever trance she was in. That breath she took remains locked in her chest for a second longer before she lets it out. She screams directly into your face, a wave of garlic and Tic Tacs, and grips you by the hairy armpits.

You're flying through the air, backwards.

You hit the fridge and slump on the floor there, dazed.

Mrs. Lautrec's screams trail off down the hallway outside your apartment. You look between your legs and focus on your weird little sloth boner, trying like hell to remain conscious.

CHAPTER SEVEN

Voices call to you from the real world. Sounds like Randy, somewhere out there, repeating your name. But you're busy at the moment.

You're down in a well, sitting at a poker table across from a groundhog with a visor on its head and a cigar clenched between its teeth. Echoes of water dripping somewhere down there. Fluorescent green lichen on the walls, reaching up toward the circle of light hovering above your heads. Leader-1 is dealing.

You look at your cards and stifle a smile because you know your full house jacks-over-eights has him licked. That little rodent has been bluffing all night, and right now he's sitting on nothing better than top pair. But you suspect he doesn't even have something that good.

You decide to slow play him. "Check."

The groundhog says, "Hey, wow, check out the neat monkey."

He sounds just like Randy, which weirds you out a bit. "Fuck you, rodent. I'm no monkey. Now, drop your bet or your cards on the table."

Leader-1 waits patiently, deck of cards clutched in his metal hand. The groundhog reaches across the table and waves his paw in front of your face. He says, in a different voice that sounds just like Cross, "Not monkey, retard, sloth."

The glass of cold water dumped on your head is not exactly necessary. You were coming to gradually and would have gotten there on your own. You know which cruel bastard is responsible. Your eyes open. The well is gone and you're back at your place. Randy and Cross lean over you. The empty glass is in Cross's hand. You reach a claw toward his face, fully intent on blinding him, but you're sloth-slow. He easily smacks it away.

Cross says, "You okay, Jungle Fever?"

Randy leans closer and pokes your fur with a finger. "Where did a sloth come from? And how is it able to talk? And why does it think we're playing poker?"

"Looks like somebody was discovered by the landlady, who didn't take an instant shining to him." Cross helps you to your wobbly sloth legs. "Which is pretty much normal, I suppose. You've always had that effect on Lady Lautrec. What'd she do, drop kick your ass across the room?"

You rub the bump at the back of your head and check out the dent it put in the fridge door. "More like a double-fisted heave."

Randy fish-mouths but can't find his words. Cross lets him struggle for a second longer before clueing him in.

"Randy, I know you have a lot of questions, and most of the answers will go right over your low forehead anyway, so let's keep it simple. This is our neighbor. He has been turned into a sloth."

"Oh my gosh!" Randy touches your face and lifts your arms, like he's trying to find the zipper to your sloth suit. "You really are a sloth! This explains so much!"

You shake free of him and stagger toward the couch. "I have no idea what any of this explains, so if you do, I'm all ears."

"But when? How?"

Cross checks the fridge then apparently remembers he drank everything that was in there. He looks genuinely sad.

"Randy, what say you make a supply run?" He looks to you and says, "How about Mr. Sloth? You need anything special?" He turns up his nose and catches the scent in the room, looks to the carpet and sees the mess you made. "How about a pack of fucking diapers?"

Randy and Cross hold their noses and inspect the carnage on the floor.

"That's all thanks to you, my friend. And whatever it was you put in my glass last night. It sure as shit wasn't just whiskey."

Cross flicks his eyes at you and says, "What? I didn't put shit in your drink. You just can't hold your liquor, like usual."

You say to Randy, "If you're making a run, I would appreciate something green and leafy. My insides apparently won't tolerate anything else, and I don't exactly have any trees nearby that I can sit in all day and munch on."

Randy can't stop stealing looks at you. "Um, yeah, sure." He heads for the door, stumbling over his own feet. "Wow," he says. "This is so trippy. I can't believe it's real."

"Yeah, you and me both."

Cross gives him a shove out the door. "Okay, chop-chop, Short Bus. Daylight's a-wasting here."

Once Randy's gone, Cross says, "Alright, what happened? How'd you let yourself get spotted by the lady of the house?"

You take a deep breath and play it back for Cross. He has no explanation for her odd behavior either, but loves the thought of her breaking into apartments so she can beat around the bush.

After a moment of quiet reflection, he says, "So, what are the chances that Lady Lautrec is calling animal control on your ass right about now?"

Shit, you hadn't considered that. The thought of being carted off to the pound contracts your sloth sphincter. "Holy hell, I can't get arrested. Don't you know what will happen to me in one of those animal jails? I won't last an hour in there."

Cross nods his agreement. "They'll eat you alive, that's for damn sure."

"You're not helping. What the hell do we do?"

Cross rubs his chin. "How about going down there to talk to her? Maybe just explain what's happened?"

"How do I explain what's happened when I still don't fully know what the fuck has happened?"

"Shit, I don't know. It's worth a shot, right? And besides, she's got some explaining to do herself, breaking into her tenants' apartments so she can slap the gash. That's not right."

You cringe at his terminology, and doubt he actually has a problem with it, but agree with the assessment. Maybe talking to her would be the best course of action. You could use a few more allies in this situation, if you planned on getting to the bottom of it.

"Okay, let's go talk to her."

"Whoa, what do you mean, let's? You're the one that's got the story to tell. I've got to get my ass to work soon. I have a full day of being successful ahead of me, but you wouldn't know anything about that."

"It will be easier to talk to her if you go down there with me. She's going to shit her britches if the scary, talking sloth that just busted her while masturbating comes knocking on her door. And you owe me one after last night. That shit wasn't cool."

"Owe you one? I got your hairy ass laid last night, and *I* owe *you* something? You're confused in that shrunken little pet brain of yours, my friend."

"Did you happen to notice my carpet? Did you pick up on the woman-shaped outline amidst the assplosion there? You caused that, with your whiskey and bad intentions."

Most of that is true, except for the part that outdated bologna played. But what Cross doesn't know won't hurt him.

He considers it for a moment and finally says, "Alright, let's get this shit over with."

* * *

Mrs. Lautrec screams again, even after Cross warned her. It takes a bit of effort to convince her to let you two in and to keep her from smashing you with an umbrella. Once she finally calms down, things go much smoother, except for the dog.

"You haven't called anybody, have you Mrs. L?"

Her little Yorkie is yapping hard, bouncing around on stiff little legs. His whole tiny body trembles, the ends of his wispy brown hair waving in the air from his frenetic energy.

Mrs. Lautrec looks at you uneasily, still warming to the whole talking sloth thing. "Heavens no. Who I am calling? I am not remembering how I end up in your room in the first place. One moment, I am playing solitaire on the iPad machine, the next I know, a chimp is slapping me and my feet smell terrible. ROBERTO, HUSH!"

Roberto the Yorkie cringes at his mistress and backs off a bit. The barking pauses for three seconds before starting up again.

NOTDOGNOTDOGNOTDOGNOTDOG

Randy passes by the open door with his hands full of plastic grocery bags. Cross stops him and searches for the beer. "This shit better be cold," he says.

"Of course it is." He looks to you and says, "Sorry, but they didn't have any of that good Weimaraner stuff, so I had to get something else."

"I don't really care, just please tell me you got something green. I'm so hungry my stomach feels like it's going to crawl out of my body and eat me."

Randy nods at Mrs. Lautrec. "How are you doing today, ma'am?" He points at you and says, "Did you see he got turned into a sloth?"

Mrs. L looks at him quizzically and says, "Of course I am seeing this. ROBERTO, SHUT UP! How am I not noticing when a creature and a lech are darkening my door?" She says to Cross, "The stupid one is your friend, yes manwhore? Is that out of some charity, like the Big Sisters, Big Brothers?"

Cross drains a can of beer and immediately cracks open a second. He pats Randy on the back then shoves him down the hallway. "Yeah," he replies. "He's our special little guy."

NOTDOGNOTDOGNOTDOGNOTDOG

"ROBERTO!" Mrs. Lautrec tells Randy, "While you are

going that way, get rid of that disgusting carpet in the sloth-man's house. Just be throwing it from the window to the dumpster below before it stinks up the whole building. And then take a shower." She looks back down at you and says, "Lord knows the diseases that crawl from this one's backside."

You take offense, but decide not to push it with more important issues at hand. "Mrs. Lautrec, can I get your assurance that you won't call the police, or animal control, or anyone else until I can get a handle on what's happening here? It's becoming increasingly difficult to explain my situation to anyone else."

"Yes, for now, I say nothing." She snakes out a hand and grabs Cross by the collar, and grips a handful of hair on your head with the other. You squirm against her surprising strength. "And the two of you perverts are saying nothing of this affair, as well. We are agreed?"

You both offer promises of your silence until she finally lets you go. "Now, fuck off," she says, and slams her door. Roberto the Yorkie continues to bark.

NOTDOGNOTDOGNOTDOGNOTDOG

"Did you guys hear that?"

Cross ignores your question and takes a drink. "Wow, where'd she get off calling us perverts when she was the one primin' the hymen on your couch?"

"Good God, really? Primin' the hymen?"

"Yeah, you know. Rubbin' the nubbin? Buffin' the muffin? Auditioning the finger puppets?"

"Where do you get this stuff, some kind of thesaurus of perversity?"

"Yeah, it's called the Internet, dipshit." Cross finishes his beer and tosses the empty your way, but you make no attempt to catch it. "Alright" he says, "I gots to work. You two retards try to stay out of trouble."

You offer your middle claw in response and start the long, slow shuffle back to your apartment.

CHAPTER EIGHT

Randy's got the carpet halfway out the window.

"Hey, your phone keeps ringing. Should I answer it?"

You consider the stain left on the scuffed wood flooring where the carpet was, and the fact that it's likely all over Randy's hands as well, and say, "Not at the moment, thanks."

Randy chucks the stinking roll the rest of the way out the window and whistles as he watches it plummet. "Oh, crap," he says. "I think the dumpster is out the other window."

"Please tell me you didn't just deposit that nasty thing on the front steps of our building."

"Hey, my bad. I'll just go take care of that real quick."

He hustles out the door while you head for the computer. Time for another email, and, hopefully, some real goddamn answers this time. After that, you have no clue what to do. You bang away at the keys as fast as you can and shoot it off. And then just sit and wait. You click around the Internet, hoping for a swift reply. You find a website with an extensive list of slang terms for female masturbation. You open your files and check the download status of Gruber's book. The PDF has finally finished loading. It only took a week. The project is due today, but you've still got two-thirds of the fucking thing left to edit. Not like you're able to concentrate enough to work right now, but you try anyway. You click the pages and muddle through the text and feel the migraine forming at the base of your sloth skull.

One chapter bleeds into the next. Time is a snake swallowing its tail. Gruber's words bore a hole through your rational mind and fill the void with useless self-help hokum.

Power animal? Mine is hyena. This does not upset me. It is how it is. I do not wish it to be any other way. Wishful thinking is for assholes and losers. Do not waste time wishing, or like saying goes, you end up with shit in your hands.

You grab one of Gruber's books from the stack on the table next to the computer, last month's payment in lieu of cash because the publishing company is going broke. No wonder, with the kind of junk they print. You check out the author photo on the back of the book. Gruber is a leathery sort who looks quite a bit like Neil Tyson-DeGrasse, minus the aura of intelligence. He's got an uncomfortable sneer for a smile and you hear him in your head as you read on about power animals.

Power animal is control. What you are represents what you control. If you are shifty, conniving politician only interested in your own survival, your power animal is rat. If you are lowly, treacherous lawyer who slides through life on own belly with the lowest forms of life, snake is what you are in essence, and in power animal. Think about yourself for a moment, and if you are honest, you will know your own power animal.

Step one is the being honest with the self, even if this leads to the discovery that you are not the good person you always assumed you were.

Step two is the accepting of that self-discovery. When you accept who you are and what you are, doors of life begin to open to your possibilities. What comes next depends on your willingness to step through those doors.

You look at your curved, yellow claws and consider the possibility that this guy's mumbo jumbo could actually be accurate. Is this really who and what you are? A slow-moving herbivore and victim of life's quick changes because you're too slow and dull to react to them? Are you the literal and figurative representation of sloth?

You rub your furry temples and contemplate your life.

How much more could possibly go wrong?

What could you have possibly done to ever deserve any of this?

Who the hell would do this to someone, and to what end? You don't have money. You aren't anyone important. The only explanation you can think of is it's all just one big prank by some sociopath. And you're the sap.

Who do you know who could do such a thing? Cross is a pretty terrible person, but even he wouldn't do something like this. That's how sadistic this monster is.

Your phone rings, and you consider ignoring it, especially when you see the number's been blocked. This can be only one thing, but you take it anyway, making sure you put it on speaker.

"Hi, this is a wrong number," you say in a bored monotone. "This is not the person you're trying to reach. That was not my penis you saw on Craigslist, and you definitely do not want to meet up with me for gay sex in the company of a spider monkey. Trust me on this. I'm not what you're in the market for." The irony being, now that you're a sloth, maybe you actually *are* what they're in the market for.

There's no response at first, and you're about to hang up, but static on the other end comes through. It's thick and mucousy, choked. Then the garble clears and you understand what you're hearing: laughter. Deep, belly shaking, lungbutter dislodging merriment.

"Who is this?"

The person on the other end is trying to respond, and failing. So is your patience.

"Who the hell is this? How'd you get this number, fucko?"

Finally, a man's voice responds. "Hallo? Hallo?" he says in a thick, strange accent that sounds like a mutation between Jamaican and Croatian. "Are you still there? Hallo?"

Your veins harden at the sound of the cackle. Your breath hitches in your sloth chest. You can't explain it, but you suddenly know exactly who's on the other end. You're certain of it. But you still can't stop yourself from whispering, one more time, "Who the hell is this?"

"I am wondering," the guy says between barking giggles, "how you are like being sloth?"

A new round of laughing/gagging erupts, and you stab a claw at the phone and cut off the call, desperate to kill that horrible, haunting racket.

Jesus, the bastard hacked your computer, and now he has your number. What else does he have? He probably knows everything about you. He'll have gotten hold of your social security number, and your bank account. Not that he'll get anything out of it. You don't bother much with the bank these days. You probably owe them money like you do everyone else.

But what was coming next? You can tell by the sound of that bastard's voice that he's having entirely too much fun torturing you. So what's his plan moving forward, because this whole mess is only getting worse, not better.

You could kick yourself in your own sloth ass. You wanted answers from this fuck, and you had him on the line. And what did you do? You shat your sloth pants and hung up. Like a scared little bitch. Like a weak-minded little animal. You cowered and hid. Typical.

"Hey, you slow little carpet stain, where the fuck are you?"

You jump at Cross's voice and turn in the desk chair to see him pushing through the front door. He strides up to the desk and smacks your keyboard, flipping it over and into your monitor.

"Whoa, easy asshole. What the hell is your problem?"

"What's the deal sending that shit to me? What if I opened that at work? You trying to get me fired?"

"Hold on. Back up a step. What are you talking about?"

"That fucking email. That hacker horseshit you clicked on like a dumbass. You sent that shit to me. And I almost clicked on it! You're fucking with my life here! I can't be turned into an animal right now. Things are happening for me, and that would completely fuck it all to hell."

You shake your head and put the keyboard back in place.

"Back off, Cross. I didn't send anything to you. You're out of line here."

He reaches for the mouse and clicks on the email icon. "I'm not out of line at all. I'm going to go in here and confirm this, and then I'm going to kick your ass."

He mouses over to your Sent mailbox. It takes a second to chew on the request, and then it finally pops open, still slow and lagging like hell, taking forever to load everything up. The two of you watch and wait, Cross snorting anger through his nose. You wonder if his power animal is a bull, but no, that wouldn't be right. He's a jackass, for certain.

"Wait a minute." He tries to scroll the screen, but it won't respond, just steadily adds emails to the top, one at a time. You look at the addresses and don't recognize any of them at first, but then a familiar one pops up: rtotheatothentothedtothey@ msn.com

"Hey, that's Randy's email," you say. "I didn't send him any email recently."

Cross points at the screen. "Look at the time-sent bar. Not only did you send him an email, you sent it to him twenty seconds ago."

He's right. There goes another one, at the top of your Sent box. And another one, with a .gov address. Christ, that one looks like it went out to a judge. Cross clicks on it, and you see right away what it is. One line that reads: *PROBABLY THE CUTEST KITTIE EVAH!!* followed by a html link. Spam email, each one containing the same link that you clicked on, the very same one that turned you into a sloth, is steadily pumping out of your account. It's some devious shit, too. Who can resist clicking on a video of probably the cutest kittie evah? Whoever's doing this is a heartless bastard.

"You've been hacked big time, you moron."

"Yes, Cross is right." Both of you turn to Randy, who's standing in your living room. "That's not the worst of it, either."

Your slow sloth mind is trying to keep pace. You stutter out, "W-what's the w-worst of it?"

He looks down at you with the gravest, most serious face you've ever seen from the normally open-mouthed idiot, and says, "You've officially been added to the Domestic Terrorist Watch List for suspicion of digital crimes against humanity."

CHAPTER NINE

You sit next to Cross on the couch, both held in rapt attention by Randy. Neither of you speak, so astonished by this sudden explosion of knowledge and change in demeanor from your mild-mannered and dim-witted neighbor.

Randy says, "Have you been noticing a lot of computer lag lately? Things won't load up or run quickly? Lots of hang-ups and lack of speed?"

You nod like a dunce.

"That's the Spammer. He's turned your computer into a zombie."

"He has?"

"Yes, he hacked into your machine several months ago. Installed a program called a Trojan horse, probably through something you downloaded from the web or an email. It lies dormant for weeks, sometimes months, until it's programmed to turn on and take over your machine. Now that it has, he's got access to everything in your computer, and he's using your system as a twenty-four hour spam email dispenser. He's been on our radar for some time. You're not the only one this has happened to, but this situation is different. He's stepped up his game to something else entirely."

Cross finally finds his words and says, "How the hell do you know all of this? Are you one of those savants? Like, an unassuming genius with computers who's a social half-wit?"

"It's my job to know this," Randy says. "I work for the Department of Homeland Security."

Cross hoots and jumps to his feet, begins to pace around

the room. "Holy motherfucker!" He turns back to Randy. "I mean, what? How? When? No... You? Really?"

Randy ignores Cross and focuses on you. "Just this morning, your computer became the largest distributor of spam in the continental United States."

Your sloth hole puckers. "You can't be serious. Who the hell is this person and why is he doing this to me?"

"I'm dead serious. And the person responsible is known only as The Spammer. He's been around for years, running a number of different scams and hacks. We've been working on that link you opened in the email, and so far we haven't found out much about it. It's not an Internet link, so we can't trace it back through the web."

"So then why not shut the fucking thing off?" You jump down and wobble toward the desk, but Randy steps in front of you and says, "No, we can't do that."

"Why not?"

"I don't want to disrupt the only link we have that leads back to The Spammer."

"Fuck that shit! Shut it down!"

Randy exhales and picks you up, sets you back on the couch. "This is an active investigation. I'm only telling you all of this because I know you're innocent. I've been watching you for some time now and I know you're not part of this, but my CO thinks otherwise, and that's why you remain a suspect."

"WHAT?"

"Yes, which is why we need to prove you have nothing to do with any of this. My assignment was to find the connection between you and The Spammer, or to prove that you *are* The Spammer, but I'm convinced you're not a criminal. You're a dupe for a criminal. And now you're a ..." He looks at Cross, who rolls his eyes and says, "Sloth. He's a fucking sloth."

"Right, a sloth. I knew that. That's a kind of monkey, isn't it?"

You're up and pacing the couch, climbing onto the window

frame, suddenly exploding with nervous energy. "This is nuts! What can I do?"

"Again, I'm working on it, but I need your help. We're running out of time. Something big is in the works and it's going to happen soon. DHS won't wait much longer to move on you, whether I tell them to hold off or not. The Spammer is setting you up as the fall guy, and by the time any of this gets sorted out, he's going to be long gone."

"How do you know that?" Cross says. "You don't even know where the guy is, or what the hell he's up to. Right?"

Randy shrugs and mumbles some half-hearted response. You don't quite hear what he's saying because you're climbing the furniture and about to jump out the window.

"That's what I thought," Cross says. "Fuckin' government employees." He points at you. "What the hell are we supposed to do with him, huh? Just let the spooks come in and haul him away? He got turned into a sloth! He's a victim here, not some cybercriminal mastermind! Look at him for fuck's sake!"

"Yeah man, I need to get the hell out of here." You hurry over to Randy as fast as your sloth body will move and pull on his arms and clothes. "Come on, get me out of here. Don't let them arrest me. I'm an innocent sloth. They'll stick me in the zoo with real sloths who'll know I'm a fraud. Or they'll put me in a cage with a bunch of stray dogs and shit, and they'll rip me to pieces. I'm not cut out for prison, man. I'm too tender. I won't last a second in there!"

You've climbed straight up Randy's front and crawled over his head, and now you're working your way back down the other side. You're coming out of your fur. This can't be happening! You didn't do anything to deserve this!

"You guys have to hide me."

Cross shoves Randy and says, "Come on, dummy, fix this. We gotta help him."

"Please, don't lay your hands on me. I'm a government official."

"You're officially a government asshole, and you need to make this shit right."

Randy turns on Cross and gives him a shove back. "I'm open to suggestions, okay. This Spammer asshole has been on the lam for years. It's not like I can just call in a raid and take him down whenever I feel like it. These guys move all over. It's likely he's not even in this country. He could be anywhere in the world right now. All he needs is an Internet connection to pull this stuff off. So unless you have some great plan you're willing to share, back off and quit pushing me, you big jerkhead!"

Cross sticks a finger in Randy's face. Opens his mouth to say something but pauses in mid retort and looks at you. "Wait, didn't you say he emailed you back once already?"

You nod and begin to rock on your sloth butt, trying your best not to go tear-assing and screaming around the apartment again. That probably won't help matters at this point, but it would feel better than this sensation of the world crashing down on top of you. You head for the kitchen and root through the fridge for beer. The hell what it does to your guts, you need a drink.

Cross says, "Okay, how about sending this prick another email? He's already responded to you once, so he's liable to do it again."

You slug down half a can of beer and belch. Then you say, "And he called me, too."

Randy bug-eyes you and shouts, "He what?"

"Yeah, just before Cross came in. I totally freaked when I realized it was him. I thought it was another one of those Craigslist guys who can't dial a phone right, but the bastard just started laughing at me, asked how I liked being a sloth. Smug son of a bitch."

"Did you get a phone number?"

You shake your head as you toss your empty can on the floor and go for another one. "The number was blocked."

Cross walks over and gets a couple beers for himself,

tosses one to Randy, who grabs it and picks your phone up off the desk.

"I'll get CPD on this. I have an asset in the department. We'll check your phone records and try to trace the incoming number. It probably won't lead anywhere, but it's a start."

You'll take that right now. You like clues and starts. Those are good things. You also like beer, and that first one has quite nicely taken the edge off the situation. Your immediate plan now is to slowly drink yourself into a stupor. That sounds agreeable. Just drift away from all this. Let the humans handle it. You're a sloth. You're not capable of doing any of this crap.

The knock on your front door snaps you back to reality. "Shit, is this it?" You scramble behind Randy's legs. "Is this the raid?"

Cross opens the door and lets Mrs. Lautrec in. "Cops don't usually knock gently at the front door on a raid, fur brain. They knock the fucker down."

Mrs. L glances nervously around at each of you. "I was... just in the neighborhood."

Randy says, "Mrs. Lautrec, were you eavesdropping on our conversation?"

She nods fast, embarrassed. "Yes, I'm sorry. I don't mean to be nosy old lady. But I hear what you talk about and I get the email, too." She points at you. "From the sloth-man."

"You didn't click on it, did you?"

Cross tosses Mrs. Lautrec a beer, and she snatches it from the air with a surprising deftness. She pops it open and chugs as Cross says, "Look at her. Does she look like a sloth?"

Mrs. L says, "I don't remember. I have felt strange all day. Something happened, but I do not remember."

Cross opens his mouth to say something, almost certainly another crude reference to masturbation, and you cut him off to save Mrs. Lautrec the embarrassment. "And we're not going to discuss it, either. Right guys?"

Cross looks disappointed but agrees. He picks up one of

Gruber's books from your desk, flips through the pages and grunts. "Man, you read some dumb shit."

"Now," you continue, ignoring his remark, "can we please do something else that will in some way move this along?"

Randy sits at your desk. "Yes. Let's start with another email. See if we can coax this Spammer into doing something that we can trace. Maybe we'll luck out and he'll—"

Your ringing cell phone cuts Randy off and all of you stare at it. The display shows a blocked incoming number. Randy sets it on the floor in front of you and prepares to connect the call.

"Okay," he says. "This might be our last chance to talk to this bastard. Keep him on as long as possible."

You nod and try not to fart. The beer is beginning to work through your still-shaky sloth plumbing. You crack your sloth knuckles and take a deep breath.

"Let's do this shit."

Randy hits the button, and you say, "Hello?"

Nothing. Just breathing on the other end. Shallow respiration, like he's been running.

"Hello," you say again, trying to keep the nervous rattle out of your voice.

Another long, unendurable pause on the other end, and then, finally, a reply. "Uh, hello?"

It's not the same voice. It's higher this time. From the smaller lungs of a smaller man.

"Who is this?"

Silent pause. Huffing breath. Your sloth heart blasting in your sloth ears. "Yeah, um. I'm calling about the ad? This is Dickie."

The pent up anxiety and frustration gush from you in a tidal wave of obscenities that makes Cross smile. He looks almost proud. Mrs. Lautrec turns a deep shade of burgundy beneath her coat of blush.

You're about to throw the phone through the wall, but Randy stops you.

"No! Don't destroy the phone. We need it just in case the Spammer actually does call back."

You're seething, on your hands and knees, crawling around like the beast you've become. Randy turns back to the computer to work on the email. Cross returns to the Gruber book he's paging through. Mrs. L gives you a look and stoops down by your side. She feels sorry for you and strokes your head, which feels quite nice and instantly calms you.

Cross says, "You know, you can always just remove your ad from Craigslist."

Once your breathing has normalized, you say, "That won't stop these guys from accidentally dialing my phone number, though."

"So how about you call this other dude and ask him to change his ad?"

You're about to tell Cross that's a really stupid idea, but you stop and think about it for a second. It's actually not half bad. "Well, maybe. Worth a try, I suppose."

Cross walks over to the desk and picks up the phone. Randy tells him, "Okay, but do it fast. We don't want to miss the Spammer if he tries to call back. We need to keep that line open."

"Relax, government tard, that's the whole point of calling, so we don't get any more cranks looking for butt sex. We've got it locked down. You just worry about the email thing."

Cross hands you the phone without looking at you, his eyes still in the Gruber book. "Holy Christ," he says. "Do you seriously have to read through this turd's books? That's, like, your job? Proofing an asshole's nonsense?"

You carefully tap in the number with your sloth skewers. "It was, but not after this week. I was supposed to finish my latest project today, but that isn't happening. And then I'll be out of a job."

You glance at Mrs. Lautrec and quickly add, "But no worries, I'll still have the rent."

It's total bullshit, and both of you know it, but she just waves it off. The line rings as you rub the space between your sloth eyes, trying to massage away the massive stress headache forming there. The only cure at this point is more beer, which you will get to work on as soon as you finish with this asshole, who finally picks up the line and snorts out, "Hallo!"

Your mouth is open, but you can't speak. Everyone stops what they're doing and turns to you.

You can't breathe at all.

You stagger back and nearly pass out.

You can't believe it.

"Ya, hallo? Who in fuck is this? Are you call for the homo's sexual advertisement? Speak to me dammit!"

It's him.

CHAPTER TEN

Son of a bitch, it really is him. You've got him right there. And what do you do?

You hang up on him, again.

Randy grabs the phone, but it's too late. "What's wrong?" he says. "Who was that?"

You still can't find words. Cross smacks you in the back of the head with Gruber's book. "Come on, spit it out."

You sputter, "That was. Him. That was him!"

Randy says, "Who him? *HIM* him?"

"Yeah, him. The guy. The Spammer fuck."

Randy's seriously confused. "I don't get it. How did you call him?"

Cross picks you up by the neck and presses his nose into yours. "You mean that was the guy that we are trying to find? You had him on the phone again, and you hung up on him, *again?*"

"Shit, yeah. I panicked!"

"No, maybe that's a good thing." Randy grabs a pen and pad of paper from the desk. "What was that number? Ends in 1616, right?"

"Yes. And his screen name is ArmyG403. Is that a clue, too?"

Randy scribbles it down. "I don't know, maybe. Not likely. It'll just be a fake screen name. This guy wouldn't be dumb enough to use anything that could identify him. But the bigger implication is, we've got his number to trace. This area code is local. He's right here in the city."

New light dawns on you, like waking from a bad dream.

"Damn, I know how we can find him. We can respond to his ad and set up a meet with him! He'll lead us right to himself!"

Randy says, "That's it. Ensnare him with the promise of sex! No man can refuse that! It's brilliant!"

You reflect in the glow of this new development for a moment. Then Randy puts words to the collective feeling that's settling in the room. "I can't believe the coincidence, though. What are the odds that the person who hacked you and turned you into a sloth also has a phone number nearly identical to yours, runs a Craigslist ad the same time you do, and lives in the same city?"

Mrs. Lautrec makes the sign of the cross and says, "There is no coincidence. This is... *sinistre*. How you say? Spooky. Is very spooky."

All four of you fall silent and let it sink in. The serendipity of it is unsettling at the least. The more you consider it, the more it freaks you out. Cross seems to be right there with you. "Hold on here," he says as he flips through Gruber's book until he finds whatever he's looking for.

"I can't believe I'm quoting this fruit, but listen to this." He uses his finger to keep his place as he reads, "'There is such a thing as divine intervention. The source of that divinity will be a matter of your personal faith, but the results are real. Whether Christian or Buddhist or Aztec, the coming together of forces, cosmic or natural, combine to form a perfect storm of coincidence that will ultimately prove to not be coincidence at all, but rather evidence of a grander plan that was in place from the very start.'"

He looks up from the book and says, "Sounds a little familiar, yeah?"

Mrs. Lautrec pulls more beer from the fridge and passes the cans around. "You know, I have this feeling before," she says. "When you three move into this building. It all happened within a day or two, and you all three became friends right away. This never happens anymore except in the terrible sitcoms on the television, but is like you three were meant to come together here at the same time. Maybe this is why. You are here together, at this moment, for this reason."

You tingle with *déjà vu*, incredulous at the realization that Mrs. L is describing a concept you read just that morning in Gruber's new book, but paid little mind to at the time.

"Here, check this out."

You scramble up onto the desk chair and pull up the PDF. It takes a minute thanks to the new source of lag from your spam-pumping machine, but you find what you want and begin to read.

Cross leans in over you and says, "Goddamn, we're all going to die of old age by the time you spit this out." He picks up where you left off and reads aloud for the rest:

"'This is what I call the concept of the Significantly-Less-Than-Super-Hero. When you find that thing inside yourself, that essence which also determines your power animal, you can begin down this path. Do not fool yourself: it will not be something great, or even something good, but it is the something that makes up your you-ness.' What the fuck is 'you-ness?' This guy's as retarded as Randy."

You have little patience for his crap right now. "Please, just read and save the asshole commentary for the DVD extras."

He goes on: "'No one can be true super hero. This is not a comic book world. Everyone wishes to be savior of the day, just as everyone deludes themselves that they would be lion for power animal, because they fantasize of being king of the jungles. No, this is not the way it is. You are not a super hero, and most likely you are not even a slightly remarkable hero. You are regular person. The world is full of regular person, and you are one. Do not listen to the Dr. Feelsogood who tells you otherwise; you are not special. You will be significantly less than super hero, but that does not make you incapable of accomplishing things. You have something that can be used to an advantage. Find your dominant trait, your prevailing quality, and make it your strongest asset. Figure out what you are and how it makes you *you*, and apply that to everything in your life. Even if this means you are not jumping the buildings in the single bound.'"

Cross leans back, and you turn in your seat to face everyone.

"Son of a bitch, this guy is right," Cross says. He points at you and continues, "You're a sloth. That's your power animal. That's your significantly-less-than-super power, your manifest laziness." He points at Randy. "And his blinding stupidity is his dominant trait. That's his power. This totally fits."

"So what's Randy's power animal? A unicorn?"

Cross shrugs and eyeballs Randy. "Maybe. Or probably just some overbred dog. He reminds me of a really stupid Labrador."

Randy fires back, "What about you? Your dominant trait would have to be your assholeishness."

Cross nods, excited now. "You're right! I'm a huge asshole. And that's my advantage. I just harness it to accomplish whatever I want!"

You snort and say, "You've got a great start on it. At least the asshole part."

Randy looks at the computer screen and reads, "'Significantly-Less-Than-Super-Hero.' Check it out, SLTSH. That spells sloth!"

Cross smacks him upside the head. "No it doesn't, retard."

Randy reads it again and tries to work it out. But you've already decided - you're going to run with it, because fuck it. Close enough.

You are sloth.

PART II:
THE SIGNIFICANTLY-LESS-THAN-SUPER-HEROES

CHAPTER ELEVEN

Cross mulls it over while draining another beer. You're on your third and still standing, which is a good sign. Might be growing into this whole sloth thing a little.

He ticks off the points you made, one at a time. "Okay, first, I've got nothing better to do. Which is false. I've got a job, unlike you losers."

Randy says, "Hey, I have a job."

"A real job, douche. You're a government employee. That's not real, honest employment. Okay, moving on. Second, you say I should do this because there's a chance I get to beat somebody's ass. I won't argue that point. Free reign to beat someone's ass without legal constrictions and whatnot would be awesome, and should have been your first point."

"My mistake."

"Third, I should do this because I have a car."

He falls silent, and you tap your claws on the top of your beer can. "Well? What say you?"

"Let me ask this. Why not just call Randy's bosses at Lameland Security and tell them everything? Let them handle it?"

You look at Randy, but he didn't hear the question. He's looking at Gruber's book and excavating a foreign body from his right nostril. You point at him and say to Cross, "Let me get this straight. You want to rely on the people who chose to hire this man to help protect the country from terrorists?"

Cross is out of arguments. "You make an excellent point. Alright, I'm in based on number two alone. Let's go fuck this guy up."

"What about a name?"

"What about a fucking name? This isn't some seventh grade club we're forming here. Have you heard nothing I've said about this super hero bullshit? Hell, even your dumb guru says the same thing. There aren't any fucking super heroes."

Randy pipes up. "Sloth Squad. We can be the Sloth Squad."

You like it and say, "Seconded. We have a majority, so the motion is carried."

Before Cross can further complain and insult you, everyone jumps at the hard bark of knuckles against the front door. There's a short pause, and then a second knock, more forceful this time. It's definitely not Mrs. Lautrec out there again. Cross tiptoes to the door and checks the peephole.

He whispers, "Shit, it looks like a cop."

"How can you tell?" You ask this as you back away, looking for somewhere to hide.

"Well, he's got a cheap coat, about fifty extra pounds and a bad disposition." He turns and tells you, "Relax, just act like a dog or something and we'll get rid of him."

Randy drops to his hands and knees and tries to sniff your ass.

"Goddamnit, retard, I was talking to the sloth."

"Oh, right. That didn't make a lot of sense when you said it."

Randy stands up and you drop down to all fours as Cross opens the door. The cop looks him over quickly then eyeballs Randy up and down. He says, "Afternoon, I'm Detective Sommerset from CPD. I'm looking for a Mr. ... What the hell is that thing?"

He's pointing at you, and you offer a half-hearted bark that sounds more like a cough. Cross gives you a pleading look and turns back to Sommerset. "Yeah, that's Lenny. He's one of those mentally deformed mutts from the pound. Our neighbor, who has a very good heart but a poor set of decision-making skills, has been fostering the poor beast. Pretty retarded looking, isn't it?"

"I thought they just euthanized those things so they can't spread their bloodline to healthy dogs."

"Yeah, they probably should have dragged this ugly fucker

around back and popped a bullet behind his ear, but you know how the tree huggers and animal lovers get when you put down a few fucked up dogs."

Sommerset flips open a notebook and says, "I see. And who are you, sir?"

"I'm Christopher Cross. I live across the hall." Cross shakes Sommerset's hand. "And this is Randy the re... I mean, Randy. He lives one door down."

"Are you the only ones here in the apartment?"

"Yeah, we're just watching little Lenny while our friend picks up a prescription for the poor bugger from the vet. Seems like he's got some kind of growth going on downstairs. Like a weird, itchy fungus that he won't quit licking."

Cross winks, and you have to fight back the urge to flip him off with your middle claw. Sommerset is watching you. Cross raises his eyebrows expectantly. You curse him in your mind and vow revenge at a later date, when he least expects it, then set about angling your face into your crotch. You take a deep breath, let out an exasperated sigh, and set to licking away.

"Yeah, see," Cross says, "there he goes again. He's been doing it for hours and hours, just won't stop until he licks the damn thing right off, I guess."

You grumble, "Motherfucker," from your crotch and continue licking.

Cross turns back to Sommerset. "What did you need from our friend, Detective?"

Sommerset watches you lick for a few more seconds then says, "I need to ask him some questions regarding a couple missing persons cases we've been investigating."

"Missing persons?"

"Yes, someone appears to be targeting homosexual men in the city. We got a tip a little while ago, and it seems that several of the missing men have been in contact with your friend."

Cross turns and gives Randy a fuck-you sort of look and says, "A tip, eh?"

"Right, a tip. We were checking into your friend's cell phone account for an unrelated matter, and we discovered a large number of incoming phone calls from several of the men who are currently missing."

"Wow, that seems like a huge coincidence," Randy says with a nervous laugh.

"I don't really believe in huge coincidences, sir. There are small coincidences, and then there are connections. That's what I'm here to investigate."

Randy smiles at Cross, who shoots poison darts from his eyes. He says, "Well, unfortunately, our friend is out, and we were just about to leave as well, Detective. Thought we'd take this little guy to the dog park, try to get him some socialization time with other dogs. Thinking maybe what he needs is to just get laid by some big Doberman. I wish we could help, but I'm not sure when our friend will be back."

Sommerset hands Cross a business card. "Do me a favor and give me a call when he turns up again, will you? We really need to talk to him about this very serious matter."

"Of course, I'll call you the second I see him in the flesh."

Sommerset looks back at you, and all three of them watch as you redouble your ball-licking efforts. Sommerset says, "What kind of breed did you say that was again? Doesn't look like any dog I've ever seen."

"Yeah, he's one of those, um..." Cross looks to Randy, struggling for a good answer. "He's like a whatchacallit. A mashup, like one of those labradoodles, or some weird shit like that. I think he's a cross between a pug and a mastiff."

Sommerset's face screws up in confusion. "Who the hell would try to cross breed a tiny little pug and big ass mastiff?"

"Well, as you can see, it didn't turn out well. I'd bet dollars to donuts the breeder went to jail for it. Or he deserves to."

"Well, just make sure you keep that thing on a leash."

Sommerset eyeballs each one of you again, like he's suddenly on to everything. You can see it in his face, which is wrinkled up. He smells the bullshit being shoveled at him. But he finally leaves.

Cross leans against the door and says to Randy, "They got a tip. Nice job, Popeye Doyle. Now we've got CPD coming for him, as well as your federal pals."

"How was I supposed to know this was all connected?"

Cross strides across the room and hovers in Randy's face. "Because you work for fucking Homeland Security. Isn't it your job to know this shit?"

"Well, I know now. This isn't a perfect science. This is investigating. Following clues and making connections, just like Detective Sommerset said."

Cross opens his mouth to reply, but doesn't say anything. You suddenly realize it's silent in the apartment and you glance up at the two of them staring down at you.

Cross says, "He's gone now. You can stop licking your balls."

You laugh it off. "Yeah, of course. Just making sure."

Cross shakes his head and says, "Degenerate."

You take the opportunity to flip him off this time. "Eat me. You'd be licking your own junk too if you could reach it. You're just jealous."

Cross heads back to the door and checks the peephole again. "Alright, we need to quit dicking around here and move our asses now before that cop comes back."

This is what you want to hear. You have to get out of this apartment and do something proactive before you lose your mind.

"What's the plan?" Randy says.

Cross pulls out his car keys and shakes them. "Let's go find this Spammer fuck."

You scoot toward the door. "Fuck yeah! To the Slothmobile!"

Randy picks you up and drops you on his hip. Cross shakes his head. "Absolutely not. We're not calling my car the Slothmobile. I told you, you watch too many stupid comic book movies."

CHAPTER TWELVE

The Slothmobile is nothing like you were expecting.

"This is it?"

Cross opens the passenger door of a 1988 Hyundai Excel and leans across to the driver side door and flips the lock open.

"Yeah, so? You have a problem with an economically intelligent automobile?"

"Well, no. I just had something else pictured. With your suits and your briefcase, I was assuming something a lot douchier, like an Accura."

Cross gets in and gestures at the two of you to do the same. Randy helps you into the backseat then lowers himself into the front. You assess the landscape back there, a mess of maps, sandwich wrappers from Vito's Sub Boss and *Wall Street Journals.*

"This car and I have seen a lot together. It's paid off, it gets great gas mileage, and I can use the money I save for chasing tail. I say it's a sound investment, and I don't need a nice car to get pussy. That's what my dick is for."

"As you like to say, I'm not judging, just observing." Amid the garbage in the back is a visor for Vito's Sub Boss. There's also a nametag pinned to it bearing the word CROSS.

You're about to mention it when Cross says, "Randy, you make the call."

Randy has your phone in his hand, preparing to dial. "Okay, but we have to be on the same page here. This Spammer is clearly a very dangerous person, and also very clever. He's developed a computer virus that can turn people into sloths and he's kidnapping gay men. We need to take extra care here not to tip him off that we're onto him, or he'll be gone and we'll never see him again."

"Okay, then it's up to you to convince him that you're a horny queer who likes to fuck in front of cheetahs, and truly wants him to slap you in the face with his bulging cock. Sounds like a task that's right up your alley."

Randy looks back at you and takes a deep breath, then hits redial and holds the phone to his ear. "It's ringing."

"Don't fuck this up."

Randy shushes him and says in a surprisingly effeminate voice, "Hello, I'm calling about your post on Craigslist? I was... Well, yes, I... Dirty gay sex sounds very nice. When... I see. Yes, your, um, cock does look very scrumptious. Can we meet... What would I like to do with your cock?"

Cross punches him in the arm and whispers, "Come on, act gayer or you're gonna fuck this all up."

Randy swats him back. "I would like to take your cock and... put it in... my butthole, and... not use any lubrication, because I like it, um, rough... back. I like it roughback."

Cross smacks Randy in the back of the head. "Are you trying to say bareback? What the fuck are you talking about? You're the worst homosexual in the world."

Randy shoves him and they slap fight. You try to smack Cross, but your reflexes are much too slothy, so instead you knock the phone from Randy's hand. He scrambles to pick it up from the floor. Cross shoves you back onto the seat and whisper-yells, "Nice going dipshit! You're gonna blow this whole fucking thing, and we're doing it to help you!"

"Fuck you, let him talk."

Randy says, "Oops, sorry. Uh, I got so hot just now that my arm bumped my erection and I dropped the phone. You what? You want me to keep going?" Randy looks at both of you with pleading eyes, begging for help.

You whisper, "Tell him you want to choke on his pole and gargle his spunk."

Cross adds, "Tell him you want to suck him so dry, he'll need an I.V. after you're done."

Randy says, "I want to... choke on your pole and drink your stuff until you need an I.V. when it's done."

Cross closes his eyes and pinches the bridge of his nose in frustration. Randy listens for a minute. His eyes grow wide. He straightens the pad of paper on his knee and writes while he nods his head.

"Yep, okay. Got it, yep. I think I know where that's at. Isn't Catalpa a one-way street? Northbound, gotcha. OK, I'll see you soon." He tries to pull the phone from his ear, but slaps it back against his head and keeps nodding. "Right, yep. I do, it sounds so... hot. Yes, when I get there you can ... taste my dirty button. Right... Oh yes, I love... four fingers and a thumb in my hole. It's a very roomy space so that shouldn't be a problem... Bring a what? Do I have a groundhog? Is that, like a euphemism? Oh, you mean an actual groundhog. Well, I'm sure I can get my hands on one, if you want. Alright then. Uh-huh. I can't wait, either. Bye-bye now."

He tears the phone from his head and cuts off the call. He stares out the window for a moment and then shudders violently.

Cross says, "Okay, you got it then, right?"

"Yeah, he wants to meet at this place on Catalpa. Got the address and everything. Says to go right in through the front office and he'll be in the back. Waiting for me."

Randy turns in his seat. He looks shell-shocked, his pasty face like rising dough. "He wants to put his fist inside of my bottom while he pets my groundhog. He said he's going to shake hands with my prostate. I don't think I understand what any of that means."

"That means we got the prick," Cross says as he turns the ignition. The car rattles and rumbles to life, sounding like it could use a tune up and a new muffler. "Let's get over there and fuck his shit up."

Cross pulls away. You choose this moment to get back at him for the crotch-licking incident. You hold up the visor for him to see in the rearview mirror. "Hey, what's this?"

Cross's neck and ears burn red. He reaches in the backseat, tries to snatch the hat from you, but you crawl out of his reach. You slip the visor onto your sloth head and say, "What's the matter? Was I not supposed to find this?"

He gives up and concentrates on the road, mumbling and fuming. Randy says, "Isn't Vito's Sub Boss the place where the delivery drivers all dress up like mafia hitmen?"

Realization dawns and you can't contain yourself. "Oh, now I get it," you say, nice and slow and mocking. You're going to enjoy this. "That's why you wear a suit everyday and work downtown and drive a late 80s Hyundai and live in a shitty midtown apartment. You're not a boiler room stockbroker, or a poorly-paid first-year attorney, or an entry-level pharmaceutical rep. You're a delivery driver for a gimmicky sandwich shop."

Cross shows you his middle finger, his eyes locked on the road in front of him.

"Do you have to talk to the customers with a fake Italian accent? Have you gone to the mattresses with Jimmy Johns yet?"

Randy chimes in with, "My favorite is the *You Broke My Heart Alfredo Chicken* footlong on sourdough."

"Let's see how hard you'll be laughing when that Spammer prick is up your ass to his elbow and I'm not there to bail you out."

You toss the visor on the seat. "Come on, don't be such a baby. I don't know why you didn't just tell us where you really work in the first place."

"Whatever. Fuck both of you. I won't be there forever. It's temporary until I find something better. I got networking opportunities up the ass from this job. It'll pay off, and then I'll be laughing at you two dickheads."

Randy says, "Relax, no one's laughing at you. We're just giving you a hard time because you put on all these airs like you're some kind of bigwig."

"Right, if you'd just act like a regular guy, we wouldn't fuck with you."

"Well, I'm not a regular guy, okay? I don't like to sit on my ass and watch TV and get fat. I'm not going to get stuck in some dead end shit job that'll kill me from boredom before my cholesterol-choked heart does. I'm not going to marry some fat-assed chick who'll shit out a bunch of autistic kids just for the sake of settling down and having a family. Not me, fuckos."

"Wow, someone's got issues." You were trying to lighten the mood, but Cross is on a roll now.

"That's what happens when you grow up poor in a trailer park with your divorced mother and her string of unemployed prick boyfriends."

You chalk it up to daddy issues, not surprising, and decide to change the subject before Cross bursts a kidney from indignation. "What about you, Randy? How'd you end up working for the government?"

Cross cuts him off. "Who gives a shit? I was born poor, you were born a loser, and Randy was born a retard. We are what we are."

Before you can defend him, Randy smiles and says, "Actually, that's kind of accurate. Mom did lots of huffing when she was pregnant with me. I still tear up whenever I smell gasoline." He points to the sky and whispers, "Miss ya, Ma."

Then he asks about you. You take a deep breath, ready to launch into an account of the suburban hell from which you emerged, but Cross cuts you off.

"Save it for later, leaf-eater. We're here."

CHAPTER THIRTEEN

The place appears to be a warehouse that had an upscale brick and stone façade added to blend in with the nice neighborhood. Up the alley side of the building, there's a loading dock and side door, and the entire place appears to take up a whole block. The front entrance is devoid of any identifying mark or company logo or sign, just the address on the glass front door.

"What homo wouldn't just die to come here for unprotected sex with a sketchy stranger, surrounded by wild animals?" Cross grabs Randy's arm before he can get out. "You have a gun, right?"

Randy shakes his head. "They wouldn't issue me one. Something about public safety, blah-blah-blah. I do have a badge, though."

"Cool, they still have those little machines outside the Briteway? Did you get a concrete gumball and a pack of E.T. trading cards, too?"

You can't help yourself and pile on with Cross. "Sweet, did you get a sheet of bubble stickers for your sticker book? They just came out with some rad Ghostbusters ones."

Cross looks back, and you both say at the same time: "I've been slimed!"

Randy gets out and stomps across the street. He throws open the door and disappears inside, leaving the two of you to laugh until it goes on for a little too long. Then you're just left with uncomfortable quiet while you sit and watch the building, waiting for something to happen. After a long period of uncharacteristic silence, Cross finally says, "He went in there

a little pissed. We probably should have figured out some kind
of way to signal each other if some shit goes down."

"Yeah, that would have probably been a good idea. Maybe
he's in there right now, duking it out with that bastard, and we
have no way to know he needs help."

Cross has a hand on his door handle, getting ready to jump
out and check on Randy, when a hard knock on the driver-side
window makes both of you jump and scream like girls. Once
the terror subsides, a different sort of dread sets in. Detective
Sommerset is standing next to the car, his hand inside his
jacket like he's preparing to draw down and fuck some shit up.
He glances at you, but his attention is mainly on the front seat.

"Keep your hands where I can see them." A shadow falls
across the backseat. You notice the uniformed officer behind
Sommerset, his hand very conspicuously resting on the butt of
his sidearm. A second officer edges up the sidewalk along the
other side of the car. This looks really bad.

"Roll down your window, nice and easy."

Cross leaves his right hand on the steering wheel and
cranks his window down with the left.

Sommerset barks at him, "Your name's Cross, right?"

Cross jerks back like Sommerset smacked him. "Yeah.
Why?"

"Funny thing, that. Just after I got done meeting you and
your friend, Randy, I get a call from somebody at the station.
Something about two girls who filled out a rape kit. Says a
guy dressed like Sonny Corleone slipped something in their
drinks and took them back to his apartment and forced them
to have sex." Sommerset looks at you in the backseat, lounging
all slothlike. "With a 'retarded monkey,' according to their
statement."

shitshitshitshitshit

"And as luck would have it, same building as the place I
just called in from."

fuckfuckfuckfuckfuck

Cross shrinks in his seat. You lean next to his ear and whisper, "Please tell me you didn't roofie those poor girls last night."

Sommerset motions for the uniformed officers to move in. Cross turns his head and whispers back, "It's science's answer to the pickup line. I was just trying to move the sexual timeline up, get you out of your sloth funk."

"Screw you! Don't pin this shit on me!" Sommerset is looking right at you, but you're in full panic mode now, whisper-yelling and flinging sloth spit into Cross's ear. "You asshole! We're going to jail! They're gonna put me in the pet penitentiary! Dickhead!"

The cops pull Cross from the car and slap cuffs on him. A third cop moves toward the backseat with one of those long stick things with the metal ring at the end, like you're a rabid dog. He gently eases it into the backseat and loops it around your neck. You're too petrified to do anything besides urinate on Cross's backseat. He sees it and says, "Hey, come on! You're cleaning that shit up!"

The cop with the stick says, "Detective, this isn't a dog. I think it's a three-toed sloth."

Sommerset ignores you and focuses on roughing Cross up as he shoves him into the back of his nondescript but totally conspicuous cop sedan. "I don't give a shit what that thing is. Take it to animal control. If it gives you any problems, shoot it in the goddamn head for all I care."

Cross and Sommerset drive off with a squeal of tires and puff of blue smoke. You look to the warehouse in your panic, but there's no sign of life. Randy's inside, quite possibly being anally raped by The Spammer. This was such a bad idea.

The cop tries to walk you along with the lead bar, but you can only go as fast as your sloth legs will carry you. The other cop is impatient and he lifts you in the air with the stick, cutting off your air. You writhe against the metal loop cinched around your throat as he wrestles you into the back of their cruiser, but not before you deposit an intestine's worth of sloth poo on his shoes.

"Son of a bitch!"

The pooped-on cop leans into the back seat and jabs you with his nightstick. It hurts. A lot. You cry fat sloth tears and soak your legs with warm sloth urine. You're in a very bad place as they slam the doors and drive off. This is your worst nightmare.

They're taking you to animal control.

CHAPTER FOURTEEN

The screw with the jangling set of keys tethered to his belt tosses you inside and tells the other criminals in the cell, "You all play nice with the new kid, now."

Just before the heavy door slams home, you hear him placing wagers with his coworkers on how many minutes you won't last inside.

There's only silence for the first four seconds. You note the passing time by the thunder of your sloth heart in your sloth ribcage. Terror has wiped your mind clean, save for one final thought, the only advice you ever recall hearing about adjusting to life in prison:

On your first day in stir, shank a motherfucker in gen pop, or you'll be somebody's bitch.

But as the other inmates form a shrinking semicircle, a congealing, encompassing mass of raised hackle and hungry rumble, this doesn't sound like very practical advice. A short two dozen of assorted canines, each sporting a bowel-loosening set of personally honed prison shanks in their raging, frothy mouths, is going to consume you in under a minute. The head screw is going to win this bet.

You can do little more than make water and sit in it with your paws over your face. Just imagining this scenario was enough to give you night terrors. But actually living it out, the fear is so much worse. It's a level of fright that isn't even measurable on its own. You can't put it in normal terms. Scared shitless doesn't begin to cover the number of bodily functions reacting negatively. Your entire system begins to shut down. Darkness crowds the edges of your vision.

Breathing is laborious to the point that your chest burns and your raw throat is collapsing on itself. This is the point you realize you're screaming.

That's the terrible, high-pitched whine to which all the dogs are reacting. Snarls suddenly relax, replaced by quizzical looks and nervous sniffs of the air, as though they're sampling your insanity and deciding if they wish to get any closer to it. At least for the moment, it appears they have reached minimum safe distance.

They don't come closer, but they're not backing off either. The barking has begun. In the sparsely appointed cell, made of metal and cinderblock, the cacophony ricochets across the room and back, feeding on itself and growing. As each dog adds its voice, the next feels the need to one-up the rest.

The noise is so extreme that you don't at first pick up on the other sounds within the barking. But once you catch the first word, you focus on it. Better to concentrate on this than what is on the verge of happening; you know, the whole about-to-be-ripped-to-bloody-shreds-until-there's-nothing-but-a-smear-of-you-left-for-the-janitor-to-mop-up thing.

"DOGDOGDOGDOG"

"NOTDOGNOTDOGNOTDOG"

"DOGDOGDOGDOGDOGDOGDOGDOG"

"NOTDOGNOTDOGNOTDOGNOTDOGNOT"

Then it hits you. Your sloth ears pick up their animal talk, and you can hear these dogs speak to each other. Just like back at the apartment. Little Roberto the Yorkie. That was him you heard trying to call you out as a fraud.

This appears to be a similar high-level debate on your genus. You're not sure which is better, if they decide you are a dog, or you aren't one.

You also realize that, if you can hear them, maybe they can hear you.

You stop screaming and cough up a phlegm ball. You

stand and shake the pee from your fur. A few of the younger dogs flinch back from the spatter and launch into a round of intensified barking.

"KILLKILLKILLKILLKILL"

"RUNRUNRUNRUNRUN"

The kill crowd is definitely more forceful than the run crew. You take a deep, trembling breath and yell as loud as you can, "DOGS, SHUT UP!"

The only one to listen to you is a large German shepherd-looking mutt with a badly scarred muzzle and jagged half of a left ear. He cocks his head at you and watches.

"DOGS, SHUT THE FUCK UP!"

All but the shepherd continue to bark. You try a different tactic.

"BARKBARKBARKBARKBARK!"

Every dog stops at this and stares, every head corkscrewing just like the shepherd's. The sudden silence is almost as painful as the incessant barking. Amid that silence, a brindled mutt that's got to be close to 75 pounds ruffs quietly, and you clearly hear his words translated in your mind like telepathy:

"The fuck did it say?"

What has to be the dirtiest, most disgusting, unkempt poodle you've ever seen begins to yap, and you hear:

"Did it just say 'bark, bark'?"

Brindle says, "Wait, I get it. He's slow. You know, developmentally delayed? Retarded?"

The rest of the pack understands, and the chatter comes in from all sides. On the surface, it still sounds like a room full of barking dogs, but the urgency and anger have been replaced by a different cadence.

An extremely unpleasant looking Boston terrier says, "I thought he smelled off. Look how he sat right in his own urine. Must be hound."

An odd mix between a Bassett and a Husky takes exception to that comment. "Fuck you, Sparky."

Sparky snaps right back, "Bitch, what I tell you about using my slave name?"

"What are you gonna do about it? Sniff my ass."

The shepherd steps between the two in an attempt to keep the peace. "Brothers, please. Be nice to each other. It is bad to fight. We should work together. It is nice to work together."

You take an immediate shine to Shepherd, because he's chilling these hot heads out for one, but he also reminds you of someone. Shepherd turns to you and takes a few tentative steps closer. He barks slow and loud, like you're wearing a hearing aid.

"WHAT ARE YOU CALLED? WHAT IS YOUR KIND?"

You calmly say, "Hi, yes, it's good to talk to you. I am ... Well, I'm called a sloth. That's my kind. I'm not a dog."

You get the confused head swivels again. So, maybe dogs don't do the spoken English thing so well beyond the normal sit and stay and kill commands. You need to get through to them, and soon, before they unilaterally decide to just say 'Fuck it,' and eat you. Okay, clear your mind and concentrate on the telepathy. If you can hear them in your head, maybe this signal goes two ways.

"I am very happy to be here with you fine dogs," you say, nice and slow, in your head. "But I am not a dog. I am a sloth. Sloth."

You wiggle your three sloth toe claws and do your slow sloth walk to show them what you mean.

Brindle barks, "What kind of dog is sloth?"

Holy shit, it worked. You can communicate with dogs through the power of your sloth mind waves. You're bursting with joy at this development, but then Sparky the terrier responds, "No shithead. Didn't you hear him? He said NOT a DOG. Like I told you mutts. NOT DOG."

"NOTDOGNOTDOGNOTDOG!"

The group works into a frenzy again. A tiny Chihuahua

jumps out front, frothing his tiny rage at you. So, NOTDOG is clearly not good. It takes Shepherd much longer than you're comfortable with to calm them down again, but the crowd smells blood now. Shepherd has to wrap his jaws around the little dog's head before he'll relax.

"Jeff, no," Shepherd tells the Chihuahua. "Save your wrath, small one."

You try to help him out. "Yeah, Jeff, come on, man. Let's be friends, esse."

Jeff says, "Who you callin' esse? I ain't your fuckin' esse, Sloth."

You're clearly not helping your cause here. "Sorry, Jeff. I didn't mean anything by it. I just want us all to be cool, yeah?"

Shepherd barks to you, "You are not dog?"

Shit. You need a better answer to this question. "Sorry, no, that's not what I meant to say." You laugh and slap your sloth thigh. "Just a funny misunderstanding. I got a little nervous, guys. No, I'm definitely a dog. Sloth is my *breed*. Couldn't think of the right word, but that's what I'm called. So, you know, we're all dogs here." You look around at the wall of skeptical canines facing you. "Since we have that figured out, what time is chow? This place got anything worth shitting out the next day?"

You laugh, but no one joins you. This sell job is not going over well.

Jeff skitters forward on his stupid, spindly little Chihuahua legs. "Bullshit, this puto is lying! He's no fucking dog, yo! I say we fuck his shit up! NOT DOG! NOT DOG!"

The group begins to stir anew. Now is the time to quell this for good, or become dog food. You break out a new tactic.

"Hey, Jeff, how 'bout you go fuck yourself, you little prick."

Every dog but Jeff leans back and lets out a collective, "Oooooo."

Shit just got real with Jeff. The little bastard is spitting rage and bouncing around. He looks like a football balanced on toothpicks. "You a dead puto now, motherfucker!"

He charges. This is it. Do or die, right here.

First day in the stir, shank a motherfucker, or become his bitch.

Jeff launches his little body through the air. Your sloth reflexes respond in sloth time. At the last second, just before Jeff buries his tiny muzzle into your throat, you scream and dip back. One paw fills the airspace between you and your toy attacker. The other one covers your face, because you can't watch this.

When you open your eyes, the crowd of dogs is close around, peering down at you. Jeff is sprawled across your chest. His tiny little dog body is twitching. His stupid little tongue lolling out the side of his head, spilling drool on your arm. The three tips of your sloth claws, coated red, jut out through Jeff's spine. You feel the bones against your sloth pads and you have to hold down the hot beer vomit trying to make a curtain call.

After a moment of stunned silence, the instigating terrier says, "Holy shit. Dude just killed the fuck out of Jeff."

You roll the dead dog off and tug until your claw pulls free. Jets of Jeff's blood shoot out in arcs, and the crowd jumps back from the spray. They retreat slowly, keeping one eye on you as they move back to the corners of the room.

You're left alone with your first shanking victim, shaking and struggling to maintain the facade of your new rep as crazed prison badass.

Somewhere on the other side of the cell door is one pissed off, bet-losing screw. Any minute now, he'll be coming in to clean up Jeff's carcass, and quite possibly take out his loser's frustration on your slow ass. The dogs in the room have suddenly become the least of your problems.

You need to act again to stay ahead of this storm before it becomes a hurricane. The dogs are all watching you, waiting to see what you'll do next. The cursing on the other side grows louder. What the fuck *are* you going to do?

It hits you then who Shepherd reminds you of. He's the dog form of Randy.

"Shepherd, come to me."

Shepherd heels at your side, waiting for your next command. You can't help but laugh. You sweep your paws out over the rest of the crowd. "All dogs. Brothers and sisters. Join me now. Hear me and help me."

The dogs edge closer, still wary after the murderous display they just witnessed.

"Help me end the senseless killing that has taken Jeff's precious life. Help me avenge his death!"

Sparky, much more tentative than before, says, "But, *you* killed Jeff. Doesn't that mean we should take our vengeance against you?"

"No! Wait..."

How gullible are dogs? You're about to find out.

"It was not I who killed poor Jeff."

Lots of head twisting confusion at that. Shepherd says, "But, Sloth, we—"

"No, hear me! It was not I who killed Jeff, but *them*!" You point to the door. "Those who dwell beyond the cage. It was they who put us here, and it is they who pit us against each other. They force dog to destroy dog for their own pleasure, and they enslave us in this cage with no other intention. Tell me, brothers and sisters, when they lead one of us away from here, do we ever see them again?"

Heads turn and conversations drift through the crowd. You answer for them.

"Of course not! Those who dwell beyond the cage put us here for one reason. To control us before it comes our time to be slaughtered. And for what reason?"

Brindle's hackles raise as he shoulders into the middle of the room. "Tell us the reason, Sloth!"

What's the reason? Shit, your sloth train of thought has gone off the track. You improvise.

"Oil! Their greed for oil!"

Confusion mixes with indignation, but it's enough. It's a spark. You see it flare, and you fan it.

"No blood for oil! No blood for oil! No blood for oil!"

The dogs repeat, sort of:

"NOBLOODOILNOBLOODOILNOBLOODOIL!"

Okay, so maybe that's a long chant for a dog. Roll with it, man.

"Blood! Blood! Blood!"

This is much better. Every dog is pulled into the frenzy now.

"BLOODBLOODBLOODBLOOD!"

And none too soon, either. The door swings open. The head screw steps inside and whips open a retractable bite stick. It looks woefully inadequate next to the force you've amassed against him, but his anger at losing his bet must be clouding his judgment. He wades into the cell, letting the door swing closed behind him.

The guard gets about three decent whacks in before the pack overwhelms him. What happens next is not exactly what you were expecting. The jerk was supposed to see the angry dogs and run away. Or maybe you were thinking it would be more PG-13 family comedy-like. The dogs were going to knock him over and one resourceful pooch would steal the keys off his belt, and you would work the lock and the whole lot of you would bound off through the building while *Yakety Sax* wailed in the background.

No *Yakety Sax*, though. It's a blood bath.

How stupid do you have to be to charge into a pack of swarming strays by yourself? Who the fuck trained this asshole?

This is horrific. You just barely avoid being hit with a chunk of elbow.

There's so much blood!

Sirens scream, and a commotion of guards bursts through the door, bite sticks and pepper spray deployed to very little effect. The pack of dogs has sampled human blood, perhaps for the first time, and they clearly enjoy the vintage. Once the first wave of dogs breaks through and escapes down the hall, it's like a collective, runaway freight train. You grab hold of Shepherd's neck and swing up onto his back, clinging for your life, leaving behind a scattered line of shocked, bloodied and dying animal control workers.

"BLOODBLOODBLOODBLOOD!"

The battle cry reaches its peak as the pack surges out the front doors and races away, biting and barking and terrorizing a path through the crowded city sidewalk.

CHAPTER FIFTEEN

The ragtag collection of bloodthirsty mongrels waits around the corner, panting and dripping viscera.

The street in front of the precinct is busy. Cops hustle everywhere, no doubt responding to the call about the murderous midtown dog rampage. You need a plan. And as much as you hate to admit it, you need Cross, which is why you're here. But to get to him, you need to get inside that precinct and spring him.

Shepherd nudges your head with his gory snout and says, "What now, Sloth? What freedoms await us around this next corner?"

"What now is, we need to fucking split." Sparky is not the same wide-eyed believer in your holy Slothitude. "Every human in this city is going to be after us. And they won't be trying to beat us back with those little sticks. They're gonna blow us the fuck away with their big boom rods."

Sparky has an intelligence the other dogs don't possess, but he certainly didn't back away from killing when the bloodlust filled the air. He's a loose cannon, and he only cares about himself, which reminds you of another person you know. One asshole will be sufficient for this mission.

"The Terrier is right," you say. "We need to split up. Make it harder for the humans to track us. Shepherd, break everyone into smaller packs and send them in different directions."

Before Shepherd can act, you stop him. "No, wait. Not yet."

But Sparky doesn't stand on ceremony or sentimentality. He boogies off alone. A few of the dogs scurry away as well, trying to follow him, but the rest wait, hanging on your word. "Before we do that, I have a plan."

* * *

"Repeat after me: I will not kill any more humans."

The dogs repeat the command. Shepherd asks, "Sloth, why may we no longer slaughter the infidels who shed our blood without hesitation?"

"You just can't, okay? It just, you know, looks bad. Hearts and minds here, guys."

The dogs grumble but all agree to do as they're told. They seem to be pretty good dogs, for man-killers. They all stick to the plan, just as you and Shepherd instructed. You give the cue and they take off, raising a hell of a racket for blocks, dragging along the rest of the cops from the precinct behind them. What few police are left shouldn't be an issue for Shepherd, Brindle and the three others you kept behind.

The first cop you meet inside drops his coffee and races away down the hall screaming, a foaming bastard of a pitbull mix in close pursuit.

"Cross! Where are you?"

The building is bigger than it looks from the outside. This could take awhile, and it won't be long before the place fills back up with cops.

"Cross! Where are you, asshole?"

"Who you calling an asshole, sloth?"

The dogs jump and bark at the human, but you stop them from tearing the asshole apart. Cross looks scared and ready to split.

"Dogs, we need this human. He's not like the others."

Brindle growls and edges closer to Cross, who looks around for some way to get out of this mess he's suddenly found himself in. "Hey, fucker, tell your pets to back off, man."

Brindle barks, "All humans are alike. How is he different?"

"He's... well, he's a... He's my friend."

"He is a friend, but speaks to you in such angry tones?"

"That's just his way. His breed is called Asshole, and they have traits like that."

Brindle sniffs at Cross but backs down. "He smells like bad human. Only for you do I do this."

"Thanks, dog. Much love and respect." You tug at Shepherd's neck and command him to lead the way back out. Cross falls in behind at your gesturing, tentative and keeping plenty of distance between himself and Brindle.

You ask him, "What are you doing out here in the hall? I thought you would be locked up."

"The whole place cleared out. Something crazy is going down. The entire city seems to be coming unglued all at once."

"Yeah, tell me about it."

Cross looks around nervously at the collection of bloody dogs. "Hey, man, what's the story here?"

"These are the dogs from animal control. We seem to share an animal wave length."

"No shit. When did you learn to speak dog?"

"It's a recently acquired skill."

"That's cool. Just make sure you remind these curs I'm one of the good guys."

You discover the pit bull mix near the back emergency exit. He raises his muzzle from the midsection of the nerdy coward cop, a length of intestine dangling from his jaws.

"Holy Jesus, fuck!" Cross pukes on the spot.

"Petey!" You slip down from Shepherd's back and shake a claw at the bloody pit bull, disappointment and scorn in your mental voice. "Bad dog! You promised, no more killing!"

Petey falls back on his haunches and hangs his dripping chops. "I am sorry, Sloth. I feel the shame of the disobedient. I am weak and could not help myself."

You're upset, but you toss a slothy arm of camaraderie around his muscular shoulders. "Aw, hell, big guy. I can't stay mad at you." You scratch behind his ears with your claws. He groans with pleasure.

Cross looks at the ceiling as he steps over the disemboweled police officer and kicks the exit door open, setting off a blaring alarm. You remount Shepherd and emerge into the alley alongside the building.

Cross gulps the fresh air and wipes corny chunks of vomit from his chin. "Alright," he says in a shaky voice. "Let's get back to that goddamn warehouse and save Randy's stupid life."

* * *

Within two blocks, the neighborhood between the police precinct and the warehouse, which Cross figures to be about a mile to the north, begins to change. Tightly-packed row houses and shops begin to spread out a bit and the quality of architecture and workmanship of the brownstones improves drastically with each street crossing. Large silver maples and flowery cherry trees line the way between the street and sidewalks, which also become noticeably wider and newer.

Halfway to the warehouse, you've entered a full-on ritzy zone. That's also when you see the first woman running toward you. She's in her late 30s or early 40s, quite attractive from afar, but growing noticeably older and more professionally enhanced in the forehead and chest area as she nears. She passes the pack of bloody, stray dogs, sloth, and sweaty, wild-eyed man without so much as a sideways glance at you. She's already got terror in her face and panic in her throat.

Something much worse than your crew has her busting ass the other way. Not far behind her and catching up fast is a Hispanic lady with a set of massive breasts held back by a gray maid's uniform. You note that her sensible, thick-soled maid shoes are much better suited for running than the rich lady's shiny, black heels.

Then it's like Mark Wahlberg on the *Andrea Gail* with George Clooney, plowing headlong into the backbreaking swell that's going to swamp you and take you down to a watery grave. It's a surging throng of men in chinos and thin ties, and women who look like their noon martinis went well past three o'clock, and snarky teenagers with Beats by Dre on their heads who reek of trust fund apathy.

The pack narrows into a tight arrowhead shape, with Shepherd out front as the breakwater. You grip his fur for dear life and bury your face in his neck to avoid decapitation by Coach handbag.

"What the shit is this, now?" Cross is pointing ahead to a break in the panicked rich people. There's something else behind them, heading straight for you as well.

The first to pass by are a few cats. They pay almost no heed to the pack, until the dogs begin to snap instinctively at them.

"OHSHITOHGODOHSHITOHGOD."

You're pretty sure that was a cat talking in your head.

Next comes a huge, repulsive-looking bird with a completely bald head that can only belong to a vulture. You hear it as it passes, too.

"What is this shit? I was supposed to close on the Lake Shore Drive rooftop TODAY! Now, I'm fucked! How the hell am I flying? AAAAAAHHHHHHH!"

Two monkeys scurry by, half a dozen lizards, more cats, and several big, ugly brown rats. The snakes are the worst, and the most plentiful. So many voices in your head too, such that you almost don't realize Cross is yelling at you.

"What the fuck is going on?" He sounds strange, his voice much higher-pitched than normal. "We need to get out of here because there's fucking snakes everywhere! Fuck me, goddamn snakes!"

He dances on his tiptoes between the serpents, but they pay him almost no mind. A large constrictor type is slithering along beside a smaller, viperish-looking little bastard, and you hear the bigger snake's voice in your head:

"Goddammit, Trevor, this changes nothing. My offer was final, and your client better take it because he's looking at ten years if he doesn't."

The viper lashes out at his cohort and hisses, "You haven't

got a leg to stand on, and you know it. This puffery isn't going to hold up in court, and if Judge Sampson hasn't been turned into a damn skink like the rest of us, she'll never let this sham go forward."

It suddenly dawns on you what's happening.

"It's The Spammer," you shout back at Cross. "His big plan has begun. All those emails that have been going out from my account. These people were infected with the same virus I was, and they've been turned into their power animals!"

A Komodo dragon emerges from a spiffy corner brownstone and trundles down the wide steps to the sidewalk, joining the southward surge of animals and complaining about some sweetheart divorce settlement that's totally going to be delayed now. She apparently needs that damn thing done because boats don't pay for them-fucking-selves.

"All these snakes and shit, they're lawyers!"

Cross says, "What about that vulture back there? What was that?"

"Real estate investor, I think."

Cross shrugs as he jogs along amidst the dog pack. "Okay, I guess this makes sense."

As fast as the animals appeared on the sidewalk ahead, they've gone by, and the crew picks up speed. You pass Randolph Street and Cross points north. "Almost there, only a couple more blocks to go."

In his distracted excitement, he's nearly run over by a muscular, shirtless man wearing purple spandex and carrying a 50-inch flat screen TV.

CHAPTER SIXTEEN

Everyone has to stop and watch it. Impossible not to be mesmerized by the short, pudgy dude dressed like a doorman, punching and tugging at the half-naked guy with the TV. He's a full foot taller than the doorman, and in much better shape. He totes that huge TV like it weighs nothing, and the doorman's jerking has no effect. The guy just trudges away down the sidewalk with the flat screen plasma, his tight ass muscles exploding inside his spandex workout shorts.

But there's more. Two men step out of the next house, their arms loaded with stacks of fine-looking China plates. The guy on the right is about five feet tall and appears to be wearing eyeliner. The pockets of his perfectly pressed slacks bulge with shiny silverware, which clatters onto the sidewalk as he shuffles down the steps. His partner is a dead ringer for Freddie Mercury and sports a meticulous, pencil-thin beard and mustache. He also has a painting tucked beneath his arm. They both turn away from your mongrel pack like you're completely invisible and head north.

Dazed-looking men swarm the sidewalks on both sides of the street, streaming into the abandoned houses empty-handed, and emerging from them loaded down with all sorts of booty. A block away from the warehouse, a white-haired gentleman in a crisp slate-colored suit and red tie totes a heavy safe that looks to have been ripped out of a wall.

"Hey, that guy looks familiar," Cross says. "Isn't he that poof from the news? Anderson What's-his-name?"

"Nah, couldn't be."

But you take a better look, and yeah, that sure as hell does look like Anderson What's-his-name. Son of a bitch, it's all coming together.

"Look where they're headed."

You stop and peer around the corner of the last building before you hit the warehouse. It looks like an art gallery, very similar in style to the building Randy entered, but the front doors have been smashed and the place looks picked over inside. If it had art, it's gone now. And you know exactly where to find it.

"This is The Spammer's plan," you say to Cross. "This is why he was luring gay dudes with that Craigslist ad. He didn't want to have weird animal-themed relations with them. Well, maybe not *just* that. Mostly, he wanted to brainwash them. He's controlling their minds and sending them out to the rich peoples' houses to rob them! What devious brilliance!"

Cross stands with his hands on his hips and twists his head like a confused dog.

"Let me see if I get this," he says. "You're positing that this Spammer tool developed a computer virus that can change people into animals."

"Their power animals."

"Right, whatever. This guy also takes out an ad to lure homosexuals with a rather disturbing fetish so he can brainwash them and send them back out as an army of well-dressed cat burglars. He commandeers your computer and uses it to infect the rich people of this city, turn them into snakes and cats and shit, then unleashes the gay zombies to rob them blind."

"Yes, it all fits."

"Are you suggesting that homosexual men are weak-minded and easily brainwashed? Don't you think that's a little insensitive? If I would have come up with this bullshit, you'd have called me a prejudiced asshole."

"I would have called you a prejudiced asshole anyway, because you *are* one. I guarantee not every homosexual man in the city was flocking to this spot to have weird sex with someone they met on the Internet. Just the gullible ones. Anybody who turns to Craigslist to find a date is already highly suggestible and lacking in solid decision making skills, would you not agree?"

"I don't know. I think you're really reaching here, sloth."

"Trust me, I know. I was the first one. The Spammer tested his plan out on me and Mrs. Lautrec before setting it into motion."

"She didn't get turned into a power animal. Unless her power animal is actually a busty mature who likes to rub one out in her tenants' apartments."

"No, he brainwashed her into doing that. Don't you see? We were the dry run. Once he knew everything worked, the shit really hit the fan. And now, we're the only ones who can stop him."

"If this turns out to be his actual plan, I'm gonna be pretty pissed. This is the worst evil scheme ever, and I'm dumber for hearing you try to explain it."

The crowd of gay zombie burglars grows thicker on the sidewalk. The dogs are getting nervous, jumping out of the way as dead-eyed men toting stolen goods stagger right through the pack as if they see nothing at all. The potential to get trampled is increasing exponentially, and the dogs start to freak out.

Petey snaps at two men, dressed like extras from the set of *Party Monster,* carrying an ornately carved trunk. He runs off down the road, and the other dogs follow his cue. You strain to call back the skittish, scattering dogs, pleading with your sloth mind waves, but they've already panicked.

"No, come to me! Hear me brothers, stay! Stay!"

Only Shepherd obeys. Your Spammer battle force has diminished to just you, him and Cross. Three against a maniacal son of a bitch with an army of gay robots ready to do his bidding, and one of your group is the slowest land mammal on the planet. You need another plan, but you've got nothing now.

What you really need is a damn beer. This shit is too hard.

You aren't cut out for saving the day. It's just not in you. That's why you're a sloth. It's your power animal. Not because some sinister assbag Spammer turned you into one, but because that's who you really are inside. It's the essence of your being. A lazy, good for nothing slacker with no real skills the world can benefit from, and no ambition to actually acquire any.

You could go on self-loathing for much longer, but Cross snaps you out of your distracted fog.

"Dude, what did you do?"

"What?"

"Look around, moron."

Every gay zombie burglar has stopped in his tracks. An unnerving quiet descends onto the street. The air has changed. You can smell it.

"Why did they all stop?"

Because you told them to. You said, 'Stay,' and they did. Men must share the same mental frequency as dogs. Not really surprising, when you think about it.

Shepherd ruffs, "Sloth, what do you command next?"

You smile and scratch behind his ears. It's slow in coming to you, but give a sloth a fucking break, you know?

"Good boy, Shep."

Wait for it.

Ah, there it is.

Now you have a plan.

CHAPTER SEVENTEEN

The front door that Randy disappeared through earlier is locked, so you move around the building and try the side entrance the gay zombie burglars have been using. Cross wrestles an expensive-looking Yamaha home theater receiver from the hands of a frozen zombie that still obeys your mental command to stay.

He says to you, "If this half-baked idea gets me turned into a brainwashed gay sloth, I'm coming to rape your ass first."

He opens the door and pokes his head inside, takes a quick look around, then steps through. You nudge Shepherd. He slinks in just behind Cross as the door swings shut.

It's dark inside the warehouse, but your sloth eyes adjust quickly. Cross zombie-shuffles toward the office at the right while you guide Shepherd around the left side, using the stacks of stolen goods as cover. Cross stops in the middle of the space while you watch the office. The Spammer is there, banging away on a keyboard, his face illuminated by the glow of a computer monitor. You note the uncanny resemblance to Neil de Grasse Tyson, the odd, box-shaped afro-mullet thing he's got going on.

You've seen this guy before. You're sure of it.

He was smirking at you from the back of a book.

Son of a bitch. The Spammer is terrible self-help author Armen Lamont Gruber.

Cross recognizes him, too. He turns his head and whispers out the corner of his mouth, "Please tell me that's not the fruitcake whose books you've been editing."

You shrug your sloth shoulders. Looks like Gruber was right. There are no big coincidences.

"I told you this Sloth Squad shit was stupid," Cross says. "You've been following life coaching from the same motherfucker that turned you into a sloth."

That PDF of Gruber's new book took so long to load because it wasn't just loading, it was *up*loading. The email you clicked on was the test, and the book file must be what runs this whole thing. You're looking forward to dropping that computer off the roof of your building when all this is over. If you get out of it alive.

Gruber hasn't noticed Cross yet, and just continues to hammer at his computer. No doubt turning more rich people into beasts and dispatching crooks with alternative lifestyles. The cause of all your problems is sitting right there, the goofy-looking son of a bitch.

This is your big moment. It's time to set your life right.

It's time for you to become a super hero.

You whisper at Cross, "What are you waiting for? Get to it."

Cross takes a deep breath and lets out a long, annoyed sigh. Then he rears back and chucks the receiver across the warehouse. It smashes on the concrete floor just outside the office, showering its walls and windows with chunks of plastic and metal.

Gruber shrieks and jumps up. He storms out of the office and shouts at Cross, "Stupid homofag! What in hell is wrong with you? The semen covering your hands is make your fingers butter?"

Cross takes an aggressive lunge toward Gruber and says, "Who the hell you calling a fag? Weren't you the one telling my friend how you wanted to shove your fist in his asshole?"

Gruber staggers back like he's been struck. You guide Shepherd to the left, slinking behind the stacks of boxes and stereos and stolen furniture, getting into position.

"Who are you? How you did get inside here?"

Cross cracks his knuckles. "I'm the guy who's gonna beat

the fucking shit out of you, retard. But first, tell me something. How can a guy be so shitty both at writing self-help books *and* masterminding an evil plot?"

Gruber is stunned by this impossibly knowledgeable stranger, but he adjusts quickly, his look of shock transforming into a smarmy sneer.

"What is it you think you know? Or are you really just here to make the gay sex with all my men?"

"Actually, I'm hoping you can clear up some shit that is almost too stupid to repeat. See, I have a slow-minded friend who's convinced that you're spamming out email viruses that change rich fuckers into animals, and that you're also brainwashing queers so you can send them out to rob the rich fuckers. I told him that this is the dumbest plan I've ever heard, so please tell me my stupid friend is just stupid and that none of that is true."

"Perhaps your friend is not so slow-minded after all. Is actually a brilliant plan, if I say so myself, which of course I do because it is my plan, and I am quite brilliant."

"Oh God, I can't believe this is true. It's so lame! No wonder I didn't figure it out. I'm not retarded enough!"

"You think you are so smart? You think you are here to stop my plans?"

"I still don't get the *point* of your plans. Maybe you can circle me around the logic you're working with so I can get a better handle on it."

Gruber even laughs like a bad guy at the end of a bad movie. "Why should I waste my time explaining things to you? I should just kill you in the head now."

"Please, before you do that, just explain the animal virus part. It's the only thing that intrigues me about this entire ridiculous exercise. That actually might have some practical, real-world application beyond really shitty evil mastermind plots."

"You would not begin to grasp it even if I tried. I tell by the few minutes I speak to you that the concept would be too much for your small brain, which will shrivel and die under the power of the genius."

"Oh, I think the concept will be easy enough to grasp. Wait, hold on. Let me set my mind to think like a ten year-old with ADHD and an addiction to Adderall. Okay, I'm ready now."

You stifle a laugh and marvel at Cross's impressive capacity to be an asshole. Within a few minutes, he's got Gruber flustered and distracted. Cross very well may be the greatest asshole in the world.

"What do you know of the powers of the spirits?" Gruber's spitting now. "I have spent my life learning the arts and methods of the Buddhist and the Pagan. I am versed in voodoo and Christianity. I am an ordained priest and a mullah. What do you know of delivering the Host? How can you begin to understand the power of the mind to control other men with just your thoughts? No, I will not spend any more of my breaths on the stupid. I will simply take from them what I wish and do with them as I please." Gruber throws back his head and laughs. "Holy fuck, I am smart!"

"So, that's seriously what this is all about, Gruber? A fuckin' robbery?"

"Yes! Why is this hard to understand, even for the small-minded like yourself? Do you think what I have accomplished is come by easily? Computers require capital investment. Research and development cost money. Have you ever priced a halfway decent server farm? It is expensive being evil genius. The overhead alone will make most choose to just go straight, and book royalties don't pay for crap!"

"I can believe that after reading one of your books." Cross takes another step toward Gruber, fists curled and at the ready. "But to be perfectly honest, I don't give so much of a shit about your stupid plans. I'm just here because I was promised the chance to whip the hell out of somebody, and that somebody is gonna be you."

"Oh, you think you are such bigtime hotshot asshole. But you won't be so hotshit bigtime when I am Commander of America and you are in gulag with penises filling your butthole."

Cross takes another step, and Gruber flinches back. "Is everything about gay sex with you? Maybe this whole homophobe thing is just cover for your real desires. Come on out of the closet, Grubbie. It's okay. Mommy and Daddy will understand. Maybe not about the weird animal shit, though. You should probably keep that to yourself."

"Actually, I decide I will just kill you right now and get it over with." He claps his hands and shouts, "Faggot! Attack!"

From the dark shadows of the office, a form staggers out into the dim light of the warehouse. Randy moans and shuffles toward Cross. He raises his right arm and points a stainless steel revolver at the asshole's head.

"Oh shit," Cross says. "You gave the retard a gun? The government wouldn't even go that far. You really *are* crazy!"

This has gone long enough. Time to step in. You close your eyes and send out the vibe. Shepherd jumps out from behind a suede couch, into the low glow of the overhead lights, and you slowly rise up until Gruber can see you. He stares for a moment, trying to understand this new development. But you see him make the connection. He realizes who he's looking at and his jaw drops open.

You do a slow, cool-looking sloth point with your yellow claws and say, "Hey, asshole. Recognize me?"

Gruber looks from you to Cross to Randy and back. A hint of panic in his voice now. "Faggot, shoot! Kill them!"

Randy doesn't comply. He's not listening to Gruber anymore. He's got a sloth voice in his head, and you tell him to point his gun at Gruber. The spamming prick squeals when Randy turns on him.

"Cross, show the douchebag what you've got."

Cross reaches into the breast pocket of his shirt. He

pulls out his phone, shows Gruber that it's been recording everything. Gruber splutters and starts to whine. "Wha? Why? How?"

"Why? Because I am sloth, motherfucker!"

On your mental command, every warehouse door bursts open. Gay zombie burglars pour into the building. Gruber's head swivels everywhere, panic attacking him from all sides. The gay zombies surround him, despite his desperate pleas for them to stand down. They can't hear him at all anymore. They belong to you now.

With your sloth telepathy, you command your sexy man army.

"Fuck him up, boys!"

As was the case back at the animal control compound, this doesn't go down the way you had envisioned. No fewer than fifty men remove their pants and assault Gruber with their erections, jamming them into every possible insertion point they can find, and some new ones they create in the process. Gruber's screams last only a few seconds before three penises are rammed down his throat.

Your army has transformed from cat burglars to buck-naked fuck mercenaries. The sexual violence is mesmerizing. You want to retreat to a safe place inside your mind where you can try to process what is happening, but no, you can't do that right now. You're in control here. You snap out of your trance and attempt to command them to back off. But like with the dogs when they tasted blood, it's too late now. There's semen in the air, and your fuck soldiers don't stop until every one of them has shot his load. You catch a glimpse of Randy among them, fucking Gruber's eye socket. It's a massacre drenched in milky fluid.

When it's over, Gruber's mutilated body twitches in the middle of a puddle of blood and gallons of thick cum. Spent men stagger away and drop to the floor, slowly beginning to recover from the trance that had held them for so long.

You're numb. You finally force yourself to look away. Cross is crouched behind you, one hand over his mouth, the other still clutching his phone. He looks exactly how you feel: genuinely stunned. Finally, something has shocked even him.

"Holy shit, death by bukkake," he mutters. "That was fucking incredible."

CHAPTER EIGHTEEN

The knock on your door belongs to Cross. It's his familiar double-tap followed by the knob turn. The knock is supposed to be courteous, a grudging nod to conformity. But when he just barges on in, regardless of the response the knock draws, it becomes less an attempt at being polite, and more a confirmation of his supreme assholeishness.

It's been awhile, and you find you've actually missed him in the past few weeks you've spent holed up in your apartment. You smile at him, but then you're always smiling, so it's difficult for anyone to note a difference. Such is the dilemma of the sloth: social cues are hard to read on a slow-moving creature that always appears to be high.

"Greetings, oh slothy one," Cross says.

"Well, well, to what do I owe this honor?"

Cross walks up to the couch where you're lounging in that slothy way to which you've grown quite accustomed. He retrieves an envelope from his back pocket and drops it on the new coffee table Mrs. Lautrec bought for you. The piece of furniture was quite a surprise, as was the new rug she had delivered. She's acted rather strange in your presence for weeks now, and you're not sure what the deal is. But she hasn't pestered you for the rent lately either, so you're not pushing your luck.

"What's this?" The envelope is thick, filled with something that piques your interest. Even before he answers, you have a good idea based on the oblong shape of the bulge.

"It's your take."

"My take?" By now, you've gotten to the envelope and

begun to paw it open. Your sloth motor skills have developed nicely and you can accomplish most tasks now with your three-toed paws and long, yellow claws. They've become quite handy, in fact. "My take for what?"

"The royalties."

"Royalties? Did you go and write a book, or something?"

"Nope, from the movie."

"The movie?"

"Yes. The movie. You really haven't gotten any speedier in the brain department, have you? I thought maybe you'd develop some hybrid man-sloth mind meld, but I guess you never were that quick-witted even in your pre-sloth days, were you?"

"Hey, kiss my hairy ass and just tell me what you're getting at. I don't know anything about any damn movie. I sure as hell didn't give you permission to make one. When did you shoot this thing?"

You're standing on the coffee table, gripping a pawful of Cross's nicely-pressed Polo.

"Easy, or I'll have to call animal control." He backs away and smoothes out his shirt. "Permission for this movie was kind of a tricky beast to tame. I figured you and Randy wouldn't go for it, so I moved ahead with the project with the full intent to convince you of its merit after it was already in the marketplace. And as you can see by the bundle of cash I just dropped at your slothy feet, the marketplace has responded rather positively."

"But when? How? What?"

Cross retrieves two beers from your fridge and hands one to you, but you're not so interested in it at the moment. He admires the bottle and says, "Good to see you've finally moved on from that dog piss you bought before."

"Stop changing the subject, or you're going to start finding piles of sloth shit in very hard-to-clean places in your apartment." You flash your claws at him. "I've come to learn that these babies are rather adept at picking the cheap locks in this building."

Cross sits on the couch. "Okay, I shot the movie that day."

"That day?"

"Right, *that* day. I used my phone, and sold the video to a website that specializes in independent underground filmmaking."

"You recorded... that? And someone actually bought it? What the fuck is wrong with the world?"

"As you should already know by now, do not underestimate the powers of certain sexual fetishes. You wouldn't believe the demand for underground gay rape snuff."

"You're right, I wouldn't believe it. This is real? You have to be joking."

"You'd be even more surprised at the demand for underground gay rape snuff featuring a sloth. I call it Zoovoyeurism. It's a hyper-specific subgenre, but it pays well. Because, you know, there really isn't any of it out there. So you should be happy. You're the first star of a brand new genre of film!"

You're not sure how long the speechlessness goes on, but it's long enough for Cross to finish his beer and get through half of the one he'd brought for you.

Finally, your throat opens again. "What's this movie called?"

"It's a pretty solid title. *Death by a Thousand Dicks.* Starring Spermy the Sloth."

You cradle your face in your paws. "Aw, please tell me I'm not known as Spermy the Sloth now."

Cross smacks you on the back. "Come on, Spermy. Smile, you're a huge fucking star."

"A star in the world of underground rape snuff films featuring sloths."

"Gay rape Zoovoyeurism snuff. Everybody's got to find his niche, right? You still believe in that self-help shit about power animals and significantly-less-than-super heroes, don't you?"

There's another knock at the door. Cross answers before you can. "That's Randy. Come on in, you crazy porn star!"

Randy enters with a big smile. "Hey, guys!"

"Big Randy, congrats on the promotion."

"Thanks, Cross."

"So, are they finally letting you have a gun?"

"The promotion is really just a move to a more administrative position. Maybe once the lawsuits are settled, they'll let me get back out in the field."

You pick up the newspaper on the coffee table and look at the photo on the front page. Half a dozen serpents sit on a table in front of a bank of microphones, beneath a headline that reads: GRUBER ANIMAL VICTIMS SUE DHS

"That sucks about the lawyers getting in the middle of this."

Cross asks you, "How come you didn't get in on that class-action thing?"

"Because I think it's bullshit. A bunch of snakes got together to bleed money out of the government because the one guy responsible for all this is not alive to sue. And besides, those jerks can afford the reversal procedure while I have to get on a waiting list, and it's only going to take longer if they're dragging everyone into court."

"So get in on that, man. Get paid and get switched back so you can move on with your life, such as it was pre-sloth."

You'd thought about that. It made sense. It's what you should have done. But in the past weeks since the showdown at the warehouse, you gradually came to the realization that this is truly who and what you are. That, for maybe the first time in your life, you felt comfortable in your skin. Or fur. Whatever. You are sloth. When you're sloth, you have an identity. Before sloth, you were no one. You were just there. And that isn't good enough anymore.

Randy tosses the newspaper back on the table. "I'm glad you texted me, Cross. I was just thinking of seeing what you guys were up to. It's been awhile since we hung out. Since, you know. That stuff."

Cross produces a second envelope and tosses it to Randy. "Yeah, and speaking of 'that stuff'."

He turns the package over in his hands. "What's this?"

* * *

Cross insists on watching the video. He still has the raw file, sends it to your new iPad. You wanted so bad to strap a stick of dynamite to your old, infected laptop, but it's tagged and bagged in an evidence room somewhere in Washington now.

You try to refuse, but can't keep your eyes away from the images that remain burned in your mind. On this second viewing, you notice things that you didn't recall from the live version.

Cross nudges you and says, "Man, I can't believe what you made those poor gay guys do there. Look at Randy. You've got him fucking Gruber in the face, jerking off two other guys, and rimming that dude on top of the pile. Don't you think that was a bit much?"

"But, I didn't do any of that. I only said for them to fuck the guy up, that's it. The rest just... happened. Instinctually."

Randy shudders. His knees are pressed to his chest and he's rocking himself on the floor. "The memories come to me in dreams. My nights are endless reels of nightmare visions."

You bump Cross's arm. "Hey, you might want to turn this off. Our boy is going away to his happy place."

"They have me seeing a PTSD specialist. I catch myself dodging arcs of imaginary sperm. There was so much cum. So, so, so much cum. I think I can still feel it in my ears."

"Cross, shut that shit off."

Cross complies, albeit reluctantly. "Come on, this is good therapy. He needs to get this out of his head."

"I don't think it's helping."

You scoot to the fridge for a round of beers. When you get back to the living room, Mrs. Lautrec has joined the group. She smiles warmly at you. So much different now than she was when you were a man instead of a sloth. Your nubs tingle at the way she looks at you.

"I hear you boys from the hall and stop in to see how everyone is."

Randy recovers by draining his beer in a single swig. He follows up with a rumbling belch and says, "I'm swell. Think I'll go home and take a shower until tomorrow."

Cross follows him to the door. "Buck up, little buddy. You'll change your tune when I bring you another fat stack like that next month. And you know, you really stood out in that footage. I'm in contact with some people who think you have the potential to become a star."

They leave you and Mrs. L, who sits next to you on the couch. You show her the envelope, fan out the bills. "Looks like I have all that back rent I owe you, plus this and next month, too."

She blushes. "I did not come to visit you about money."

"You didn't?"

"No." She faces you and touches the fur on your head, petting it with long, slow strokes. "I never thank you for how you help me. You save all those people from that nasty bastard who sends the spams to my email. You are a good person."

You touch her thigh, rub your soft pad along her smooth skin. She slides her legs apart until you can see the tops of her stockings. Her breath hitches.

"You remind me of my first husband," she says. "He was swarthy and hairy too. But he was a fantastic lover."

"I'm sorry he died." No, you're not.

"I just assume he died. He left me one day. Gone to the mountains and jungles of the world to seek a higher understanding of things. He never returned."

Her cheeks redden. She looks away, and a nagging thought tickles the back of your brain.

"What is it, Mrs. L.?"

She looks back, embarrassed. She considers her words before saying, slowly, "I must show you something."

She reaches into the pocket of her knit sweater, pulls out a small photograph. Holds it close to her chest. "It's my husband. He's ..."

"Tell me." Your mouth is moving, but so is your sloth package.

She considers the photo a moment longer then shakes her head and puts it back in her pocket. "No, it is nothing. Never mind."

"That's okay." You aren't all that interested, anyway. You run the smooth back of your claw down her cheek, along her neck, over the top of her heaving breasts. "We don't have to talk."

Her breath catches in her throat. "Do that thing with your tongue," she whispers.

You slowly lick your forehead. She groans.

* * *

Mrs. Lautrec snores on the couch, wrapped in a blanket and smiling in her sleep.

You sip a beer and lean back to watch her. The world has slowed to a near stop as you bask in the afterglow. Warm buzz in your head and your slothy undercarriage. The love you made with her had been beautiful. You don't give a damn what anyone might think of this union. Life is suddenly very, very good. Why would you want it the way it was before?

You are sloth. Goddamn right, you are.

You're drawn up from a gauzy doze by the ding of an email alert from your iPad. You consider ignoring it, but that brain tickle is back, a little stronger this time. Something's bugging you, a sense telling you to read this email. You grab the tablet and pull up the app. It takes a second to fully emerge from your post-coital wonderland and grasp what you're reading.

The new email is from the Phillipino Sherriff's Attaché to East Berlin. The subject line steals your breath.

re: (SPAM: HIGH) YOU ARE SLOTH

Your limbs act independently of your mind. You tap the link and wait. The email opens slowly, an image gradually filling the screen. When you finally get the picture, you get the picture.

The image is of a beaten, bloodied sloth, dangling from a noose.

The caption beneath the image is this:

You are DEAD sloth!

Before your mind can begin to debate the what and the how of this email arriving from what you know for a fact is a very dead man, a shadow falls across the screen. You turn just in time to see the rope cutting through the air. You bring a paw up at the last second as it loops over your head and cinches around your neck.

You strain against the rope and fight for air, but it tightens and already you're blacking out. The only thing that's keeping your sloth head from popping clean off your sloth shoulders are your three sloth toes hooked between the rope and your furry little throat.

You have no hope of fighting off the attacker. Your weak sloth muscles and shitty reaction speed have sealed your fate.

You'll drift away soon. It's almost over. Unless…

Maybe you do have a chance. With one last push to keep your windpipe from crushing, you focus your mind and send out the signal.

Sloth Squad! Assemble!

You're slipping away. You're above yourself, looking down into your own slothy face. You're a slow mammal, but death comes to you just as quick as any other creature.

One final plea.

Sloth Squad, help! Fly to me, Randy!

You're out for some interval of time, unsure just how long. It couldn't have been too long, because smoke is still curling up from the gun barrel.

Randy comes to you and uncoils the rope from your neck. Air returns in heaving gulps, followed by wracking coughs that threaten to send you back under. When you finally regain your breath, heaving on your paws and knees, you open your eyes and stare at Mrs. Lautrec.

She's on the floor beside you. The nickel-sized circle on her forehead oozes blood, which runs into her eye, down her cheekbone, drips a puddle on the brand new rug she bought for you. Your breath catches again. You realize in that moment that you might have loved this woman. But she's dead now. The noose in her hand is the same length of rope in that picture.

Cross bursts into the apartment. "What the fuck was that?"

Randy holds him back. "Stay there. This is a crime scene. Can't have you contaminating it before CPD shows up."

Cross looks from Mrs. Lautrec's naked body to you to Randy and his gun. "Jesus wept! They *did* arm you. And you've already killed someone."

"She was in the act of committing a crime. I simply responded as I'm trained."

You speak up in Randy's defense. "It's true. She was trying to kill me."

Cross looks at the rope on the floor, at Mrs. Lautrec's naked body. He eyes you sideways.

"What?"

"Nothing," he says. "I'm not judging anyone. Just trying to understand what's happening. I never pegged you for autoeroticism, but whatever."

"She really was trying to kill me. Randy did what he had to do."

Cross hovers over Mrs. Lautrec's face and inspects the seeping head wound. "So, she was throttling a sloth with a length of rope, and you did what you had to do to stop her?

Shoot her in the face? You couldn't have just hip checked her and slapped some cuffs on her?"

Randy looks at his gun and runs a shaky hand through his hair. "It's the first thing that occurred to me. It was like she was attacking me, too, not just him."

"Randy, you heard me calling?"

"Yes. And it was more than that. I heard your voice in my mind, but I saw you there, too. And I could feel you struggling. I could feel the rope around my own neck, and I couldn't breathe."

"Aw, looks like you two kept your special mental bond." Cross steps back from Randy. "Just make sure you keep that other weapon of yours put away in your pants."

You slide your iPad across the rug toward Randy. "Have a look at this."

Randy sees the image on the screen, picks it up from the floor and reads the caption in the email.

"My God! This came from the same account as the original one."

"What was that you said about Trojan horses? Viruses that act on a timer?"

Randy nods fast. "Yeah, yeah. That makes sense. It must have been some kind of failsafe, in case of emergency. One last 'fuck you' to the world after he was gone. Or an attempt after the fact to cover his tracks or get rid of any witnesses."

Something still doesn't add up, but you're struck by a hunch. Mrs. Lautrec had tried to show you the answer, but you were too focused on getting between her legs. You sloth over to her clothes and rummage through her sweater until you find the photo. It's the picture of her long-lost, beloved first husband. You hold it up for the others to see.

Randy says, "Why does Mrs. Lautrec have a picture of The Spammer?"

Cross's mouth drops open. "No fucking way."

Randy puzzles a few seconds. He eventually makes the

connection. "But I thought her name was Lautrec, not Gruber."

"A dickhead like that guy, who knows what his real name is?"

"That's how he got to her," you add, finally able to see the last piece of the puzzle. "She knew the bastard all along. He must have come to the building that day. Mrs. Lautrec was the first one he brainwashed, sent her in here and forced her to play with herself, remember?"

Cross says, "Hell yeah, I remember. That shit sounded hot."

Sirens in the distance, getting closer. "So what if everyone else that was brainwashed is like this? A ticking time bomb, just waiting to explode?"

Randy's eyes grow wide with realization. "My God. All those poor, innocent homosexual men. They're out there right now, an army of sleeper cells, waiting to be activated." He pulls out his cellphone. "I have to call this into the office and let them know."

You place a paw on his leg and tug at his pants. "Not just them, but you, too."

"Aw, shit, you're right! Dammit, I don't want to be a fuck zombie again!"

Cross looks out the window at the cop cars wailing up the street. "Where the hell are they going? Five cop cars and they're all heading east."

As if in answer to his question, the building rocks and the window panes rattle in their frames. A beer bottle jumps off the coffee table and rolls across the floor, spilling its contents in a semi-circle puddle. Cross points out the window.

"Damn, look at this shit!"

A few miles off, a cloud of black smoke billows into the air. Car alarms and sirens serenade the streets below. Cross grabs the remote and clicks on the TV. Special reports on every channel. Rioting in the city. Two prominent lawyers, both still snakes, gunned down on the steps of the courthouse by a man wearing nothing but a faux fur boa. An entire city block burning from an explosion.

A news anchor gravely reads from a teleprompter: "What you are about to see may not be suitable for younger viewers. Just moments ago on the CNN network, while interviewing Michael Bobinski, a prominent jeweler who had been transformed into a brown rat by Armen Lamont Gruber, also known as 'The Spammer,' network anchor Anderson Cooper suffered a breakdown of sorts on live air and attacked Bobinski. Again, we caution you, this footage is not suitable for the faint of heart."

The footage rolls and shows Anderson Cooper pause in the middle of a question to a large brown rat. Cooper's head tics a few times and he lets out a choked gasp. Then he snatches the rat off the stool across from him, opens his mouth so wide it looks like it unhinges at the ears, and bites the squirming, squealing jeweler in the middle. The tape pauses just before Cooper tears the rat in half with his teeth.

"It's already happening," you whisper.

Cross and Randy stare agape at the TV, transfixed by the violence as recounted by moronic anchorpersons. You watch Randy to see if he suddenly snaps, but he just stands there with his mouth hanging open.

"You feeling okay, Randy?"

He touches his face, his hair, pats himself down. He slaps himself and shakes his head like a wet dog drying itself off. "Yeah," he says. "I think so."

Cross turns to him and says, "Better make sure," and slaps him as well.

Randy staggers back a step. "Nope, nothing. I think I'm good." He says to you, "Maybe having you in my head broke the spell again. Your slothy mind powers must override the Spammer's."

"You know what that means, right?" They both watch you, waiting. "We have to do something."

Cross says, "Right," and heads to the fridge for more beer.

"No, it's up to us, guys. We have to get out there and save the city again."

Randy dances in place like he's got to pee. "He's right. It's up to us. We are the Sloth Squad, after all."

Cross shakes his head and swigs his beer. "No way, that shit is done. The Sloth Squad crap was a stupid idea from the start. How many times do we have to go through this?"

You crawl over to him and grab his pants, pull yourself straight up his clothes until you're resting on his hip with your sloth arms wrapped around his neck. Your permanently-affixed sloth smile is already wearing him down. You can see it.

"Come on, Cross. Look what happened to Mrs. Lautrec. The Spammer did that, and he's not done yet. He's still fucking with us from the grave."

Cross rolls his eyes and looks at Randy, but he gets no help there. Randy holds up his gun and says, "I'll let you shoot somebody."

Cross unconsciously licks his lips. "Really? You'll let me gun down a perp?"

Randy shrugs. "What are friends for?"

Cross looks back at you again. His face cracks into an assholeish smirk. "Oh, alright. Let's go save the city from an army of hypnotized Zoovoyeurists, *again.*"

"Yay!" You leap from Cross and bound in slow motion toward the door, a slothy fist of triumph in the air.

"Sloth Squad, to the Slothmobile!"

THE END

Like the sloth, Steve Lowe enjoys leisurely pastimes like sitting, laying, lounging, reclining, relaxing, and light dozing. It's a small miracle this book actually got finished. Visit him online sometime at steve-lowe.com

Bizarro Books

CATALOG   SPRING 2013

**ERASERHEAD
PRESS**

Your major resource for the bizarro fiction genre:

WWW.BIZARROCENTRAL.COM

Introduce yourselves to the bizarro fiction genre and all of its authors with the Bizarro Starter Kit series. Each volume features short novels and short stories by ten of the leading bizarro authors, designed to give you a perfect sampling of the genre for only $10.

BB-0X1
"The Bizarro Starter Kit"
(Orange)
Featuring D. Harlan Wilson, Carlton Mellick III, Jeremy Robert Johnson, Kevin L Donihe, Gina Ranalli, Andre Duza, Vincent W. Sakowski, Steve Beard, John Edward Lawson, and Bruce Taylor.
236 pages $10

BB-0X2
"The Bizarro Starter Kit"
(Blue)
Featuring Ray Fracalossy, Jeremy C. Shipp, Jordan Krall, Mykle Hansen, Andersen Prunty, Eckhard Gerdes, Bradley Sands, Steve Aylett, Christian TeBordo, and Tony Rauch. **244 pages $10**

BB-0X2
"The Bizarro Starter Kit"
(Purple)
Featuring Russell Edson, Athena Villaverde, David Agranoff, Matthew Revert, Andrew Goldfarb, Jeff Burk, Garrett Cook, Kris Saknussemm, Cody Goodfellow, and Cameron Pierce **264 pages $10**

BB-001 **"The Kafka Effekt" D. Harlan Wilson** — A collection of forty-four irreal short stories loosely written in the vein of Franz Kafka, with more than a pinch of William S. Burroughs sprinkled on top. **211 pages $14**

BB-002 **"Satan Burger" Carlton Mellick III** — The cult novel that put Carlton Mellick III on the map ... Six punks get jobs at a fast food restaurant owned by the devil in a city violently overpopulated by surreal alien cultures. **236 pages $14**

BB-003 **"Some Things Are Better Left Unplugged" Vincent Sakwoski** — Join The Man and his Nemesis, the obese tabby, for a nightmare roller coaster ride into this postmodern fantasy. **152 pages $10**

BB-005 **"Razor Wire Pubic Hair" Carlton Mellick III** — A genderless humandildo is purchased by a razor dominatrix and brought into her nightmarish world of bizarre sex and mutilation. **176 pages $11**

BB-007 **"The Baby Jesus Butt Plug" Carlton Mellick III** — Using clones of the Baby Jesus for anal sex will be the hip sex fetish of the future. **92 pages $10**

BB-010 **"The Menstruating Mall" Carlton Mellick III** — "The Breakfast Club meets Chopping Mall as directed by David Lynch." - Brian Keene **212 pages $12**

BB-011 **"Angel Dust Apocalypse" Jeremy Robert Johnson** — Meth-heads, man-made monsters, and murderous Neo-Nazis. "Seriously amazing short stories..." - Chuck Palahniuk, author of Fight Club **184 pages $11**

BB-015 **"Foop!" Chris Genoa** — Strange happenings are going on at Dactyl, Inc, the world's first and only time travel tourism company. "A surreal pie in the face!" - Christopher Moore **300 pages $14**

BB-032 **"Extinction Journals" Jeremy Robert Johnson** — An uncanny voyage across a newly nuclear America where one man must confront the problems associated with loneliness, insane dieties, radiation, love, and an ever-evolving cockroach suit with a mind of its own. **104 pages $10**

BB-037 **"The Haunted Vagina" Carlton Mellick III** — It's difficult to love a woman whose vagina is a gateway to the world of the dead. **132 pages $10**

BB-043 **"War Slut" Carlton Mellick III** — Part "1984," part "Waiting for Godot," and part action horror video game adaptation of John Carpenter's "The Thing." **116 pages $10**

BB-047 **"Sausagey Santa" Carlton Mellick III** — A bizarro Christmas tale featuring Santa as a piratey mutant with a body made of sausages. 124 pages $10

BB-048 **"Misadventures in a Thumbnail Universe" Vincent Sakowski** — Dive deep into the surreal and satirical realms of neo-classical Blender Fiction, filled with television shoes and flesh-filled skies. **120 pages $10**

BB-053 **"Ballad of a Slow Poisoner" Andrew Goldfarb** — Millford Mutterwurst sat down on a Tuesday to take his afternoon tea, and made the unpleasant discovery that his elbows were becoming flatter. **128 pages $10**

BB-055 **"Help! A Bear is Eating Me" Mykle Hansen** — The bizarro, heartwarming, magical tale of poor planning, hubris and severe blood loss... **150 pages $11**

BB-056 **"Piecemeal June" Jordan Krall** — A man falls in love with a living sex doll, but with love comes danger when her creator comes after her with crab-squid assassins. **90 pages $9**

BB-058 **"The Overwhelming Urge" Andersen Prunty** — A collection of bizarro tales by Andersen Prunty. **150 pages $11**

BB-059 **"Adolf in Wonderland" Carlton Mellick III** — A dreamlike adventure that takes a young descendant of Adolf Hitler's design and sends him down the rabbit hole into a world of imperfection and disorder. **180 pages $11**

BB-061 **"Ultra Fuckers" Carlton Mellick III** — Absurdist suburban horror about a couple who enter an upper middle class gated community but can't find their way out. **108 pages $9**

BB-062 **"House of Houses" Kevin L. Donihe** — An odd man wants to marry his house. Unfortunately, all of the houses in the world collapse at the same time in the Great House Holocaust. Now he must travel to House Heaven to find his departed fiancee. **172 pages $11**

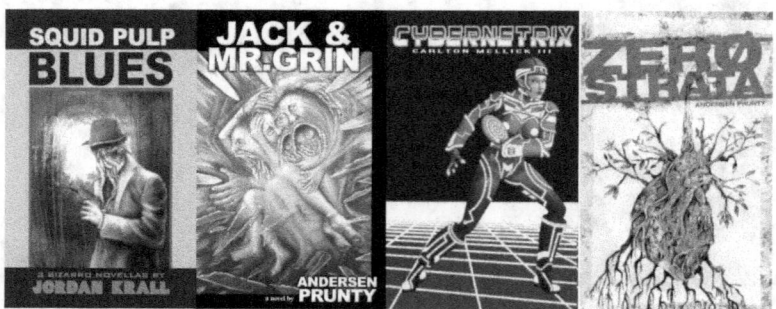

BB-064 **"Squid Pulp Blues" Jordan Krall** — In these three bizarro-noir novellas, the reader is thrown into a world of murderers, drugs made from squid parts, deformed gun-toting veterans, and a mischievous apocalyptic donkey. **204 pages $12**

BB-065 **"Jack and Mr. Grin" Andersen Prunty** — "When Mr. Grin calls you can hear a smile in his voice. Not a warm and friendly smile, but the kind that seizes your spine in fear. You don't need to pay your phone bill to hear it. That smile is in every line of Prunty's prose." - Tom Bradley. **208 pages $12**

BB-066 **"Cybernetrix" Carlton Mellick III** — What would you do if your normal everyday world was slowly mutating into the video game world from Tron? **212 pages $12**

BB-072 **"Zerostrata" Andersen Prunty** — Hansel Nothing lives in a tree house, suffers from memory loss, has a very eccentric family, and falls in love with a woman who runs naked through the woods every night. **144 pages $11**

BB-073 **"The Egg Man"** **Carlton Mellick III** — It is a world where humans reproduce like insects. Children are the property of corporations, and having an enormous ten-foot brain implanted into your skull is a grotesque sexual fetish. Mellick's industrial urban dystopia is one of his darkest and grittiest to date. **184 pages $11**

BB-074 **"Shark Hunting in Paradise Garden"** **Cameron Pierce** — A group of strange humanoid religious fanatics travel back in time to the Garden of Eden to discover it is invested with hundreds of giant flying maneating sharks. **150 pages $10**

BB-075 **"Apeshit"** **Carlton Mellick III** - Friday the 13th meets Visitor Q. Six hipster teens go to a cabin in the woods inhabited by a deformed killer. An incredibly fucked-up parody of B-horror movies with a bizarro slant. **192 pages $12**

BB-076 **"Fuckers of Everything on the Crazy Shitting Planet of the Vomit At smosphere"** **Mykle Hansen** - Three bizarro satires. Monster Cocks, Journey to the Center of Agnes Cuddlebottom, and Crazy Shitting Planet. **228 pages $12**

BB-077 **"The Kissing Bug"** **Daniel Scott Buck** — In the tradition of Roald Dahl, Tim Burton, and Edward Gorey, comes this bizarro anti-war children's story about a bohemian conenose kissing bug who falls in love with a human woman. **116 pages $10**

BB-078 **"MachoPoni"** **Lotus Rose** — It's My Little Pony... *Bizarro* style! A long time ago Poniworld was split in two. On one side of the Jagged Line is the Pastel Kingdom, a magical land of music, parties, and positivity. On the other side of the Jagged Line is Dark Kingdom inhabited by an army of undead ponies. **148 pages $11**

BB-079 **"The Faggiest Vampire"** **Carlton Mellick III** — A Roald Dahl-esque children's story about two faggy vampires who partake in a mustache competition to find out which one is truly the faggiest. **104 pages $10**

BB-080 **"Sky Tongues"** **Gina Ranalli** — The autobiography of Sky Tongues, the biracial hermaphrodite actress with tongues for fingers. Follow her strange life story as she rises from freak to fame. **204 pages $12**

BB-081 **"Washer Mouth" Kevin L. Donihe** - A washing machine becomes human and pursues his dream of meeting his favorite soap opera star. **244 pages $11**

BB-082 **"Shatnerquake" Jeff Burk** - All of the characters ever played by William Shatner are suddenly sucked into our world. Their mission: hunt down and destroy the real William Shatner. **100 pages $10**

BB-083 **"The Cannibals of Candyland" Carlton Mellick III** - There exists a race of cannibals that are made of candy. They live in an underground world made out of candy. One man has dedicated his life to killing them all. **170 pages $11**

BB-084 **"Slub Glub in the Weird World of the Weeping Willows"** **Andrew Goldfarb** - The charming tale of a blue glob named Slub Glub who helps the weeping willows whose tears are flooding the earth. There are also hyenas, ghosts, and a voodoo priest **100 pages $10**

BB-085 **"Super Fetus" Adam Pepper** - Try to abort this fetus and he'll kick your ass! **104 pages $10**

BB-086 **"Fistful of Feet" Jordan Krall** - A bizarro tribute to spaghetti westerns, featuring Cthulhu-worshipping Indians, a woman with four feet, a crazed gunman who is obsessed with sucking on candy, Syphilis-ridden mutants, sexually transmitted tattoos, and a house devoted to the freakiest fetishes. **228 pages $12**

BB-087 **"Ass Goblins of Auschwitz" Cameron Pierce** - It's Monty Python meets Nazi exploitation in a surreal nightmare as can only be imagined by Bizarro author Cameron Pierce. **104 pages $10**

BB-088 **"Silent Weapons for Quiet Wars" Cody Goodfellow** - "This is high-end psychological surrealist horror meets bottom-feeding low-life crime in a techno-thrilling science fiction world full of Lovecraft and magic..." -John Skipp **212 pages $12**

BB-089 "Warrior Wolf Women of the Wasteland" Carlton Mellick III

— Road Warrior Werewolves versus McDonaldland Mutants...post-apocalyptic fiction has never been quite like this. **316 pages $13**

BB-091 "Super Giant Monster Time" Jeff Burk — A tribute to choose your

own adventures and Godzilla movies. Will you escape the giant monsters that are rampaging the fuck out of your city and shit? Or will you join the mob of alien-controlled punk rockers causing chaos in the streets? What happens next depends on you. **188 pages $12**

BB-092 "Perfect Union" Cody Goodfellow — "Cronenberg's THE FLY on a

grand scale: human/insect gene-spliced body horror, where the human hive politics are as shocking as the gore." -John Skipp. **272 pages $13**

BB-093 "Sunset with a Beard" Carlton Mellick III — 14 stories of surreal

science fiction. **200 pages $12**

BB-094 "My Fake War" Andersen Prunty — The absurd tale of an unlikely soldier

forced to fight a war that, quite possibly, does not exist. It's Rambo meets Waiting for Godot in this subversive satire of American values and the scope of the human imagination. **128 pages $11**

BB-095 "Lost in Cat Brain Land" Cameron Pierce — Sad stories from a sur-

real world. A fascist mustache, the ghost of Franz Kafka, a desert inside a dead cat. Primordial entities mourn the death of their child. The desperate serve tea to mysterious creatures. A hopeless romantic falls in love with a pterodactyl. And much more. **152 pages $11**

BB-096 "The Kobold Wizard's Dildo of Enlightenment +2" Carlton

Mellick III — A Dungeons and Dragons parody about a group of people who learn they are only made up characters in an AD&D campaign and must find a way to resist their nerdy teenaged players and retarded dungeon master in order to survive. **232 pages $12**

BB-098 "A Hundred Horrible Sorrows of Ogner Stump" Andrew

Goldfarb — Goldfarb's acclaimed comic series. A magical and weird journey into the horrors of everyday life. **164 pages $11**

BB-099 "Pickled Apocalypse of Pancake Island" Cameron Pierce—A
demented fairy tale about a pickle, a pancake, and the apocalypse. **102 pages $8**

BB-100 "Slag Attack" Andersen Prunty— Slag Attack features four visceral,
noir stories about the living, crawling apocalypse. A slag is what survivors are calling the slug-like maggots raining from the sky, burrowing inside people, and hollowing out their flesh and their sanity. **148 pages $11**

BB-101 "Slaughterhouse High" Robert Devereaux—A place where
schools are built with secret passageways, rebellious teens get zippers installed in their mouths and genitals, and once a year, on that special night, one couple is slaughtered and the bits of their bodies are kept as souvenirs. **304 pages $13**

BB-102 "The Emerald Burrito of Oz" John Skipp & Marc Levinthal
—OZ IS REAL! Magic is real! The gate is really in Kansas! And America is finally allowing Earth tourists to visit this weird-ass, mysterious land. But when Gene of Los Angeles heads off for summer vacation in the Emerald City, little does he know that a war is brewing...a war that could destroy both worlds. **280 pages $13**

BB-103 "The Vegan Revolution... with Zombies" David Agranoff —
When there's no more meat in hell, the vegans will walk the earth. **160 pages $11**

BB-104 "The Flappy Parts" Kevin L Donihe—Poems about bunnies, LSD,
and police abuse. You know, things that matter. 132 **pages $11**

BB-105 "Sorry I Ruined Your Orgy" Bradley Sands—Bizarro humorist
Bradley Sands returns with one of the strangest, most hilarious collections of the year. **130 pages $11**

BB-106 "Mr. Magic Realism" Bruce Taylor—Like Golden Age science fic-
tion comics written by Freud, *Mr. Magic Realism* is a strange, insightful adventure that spans the furthest reaches of the galaxy, exploring the hidden caverns in the hearts and minds of men, women, aliens, and biomechanical cats. **152 pages $11**

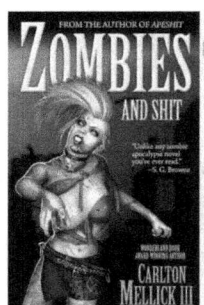   

BB-107 "Zombies and Shit" Carlton Mellick III—"Battle Royale" meets "Return of the Living Dead." Mellick's bizarro tribute to the zombie genre. **308 pages $13**

BB-108 "The Cannibal's Guide to Ethical Living" Mykle Hansen—Over a five star French meal of fine wine, organic vegetables and human flesh, a lunatic delivers a witty, chilling, disturbingly sane argument in favor of eating the rich.. **184 pages $11**

BB-109 "Starfish Girl" Athena Villaverde—In a post-apocalyptic underwater dome society, a girl with a starfish growing from her head and an assassin with sea anenome hair are on the run from a gang of mutant fish men. **160 pages $11**

BB-110 "Lick Your Neighbor" Chris Genoa—Mutant ninjas, a talking whale, kung fu masters, maniacal pilgrims, and an alcoholic clown populate Chris Genoa's surreal, darkly comical and unnerving reimagining of the first Thanksgiving. **303 pages $13**

BB-111 "Night of the Assholes" Kevin L. Donihe—A plague of assholes is infecting the countryside. Normal everyday people are transforming into jerks, snobs, dicks, and douchebags. And they all have only one purpose: to make your life a living hell.. **192 pages $11**

BB-112 "Jimmy Plush, Teddy Bear Detective" Garrett Cook—Hardboiled cases of a private detective trapped within a teddy bear body. **180 pages $11**

BB-113 "The Deadheart Shelters" Forrest Armstrong—The hip hop lovechild of William Burroughs and Dali... **144 pages $11**

BB-114 "Eyeballs Growing All Over Me... Again" Tony Raugh—Absurd, surreal, playful, dream-like, whimsical, and a lot of fun to read. **144 pages $11**

BB-115 **"Whargoul" Dave Brockie** — From the killing grounds of Stalingrad to the death camps of the holocaust. From torture chambers in Iraq to race riots in the United States, the Whargoul was there, killing and raping. **244 pages $12**

BB-116 **"By the Time We Leave Here, We'll Be Friends" J. David Osborne** — A David Lynchian nightmare set in a Russian gulag, where its prisoners, guards, traitors, soldiers, lovers, and demons fight for survival and their own rapidly deteriorating humanity. **168 pages $11**

BB-117 **"Christmas on Crack" edited by Carlton Mellick III** — Perverted Christmas Tales for the whole family! . . . as long as every member of your family is over the age of 18. **168 pages $11**

BB-118 **"Crab Town" Carlton Mellick III** — Radiation fetishists, balloon people, mutant crabs, sail-bike road warriors, and a love affair between a woman and an H-Bomb. This is one mean asshole of a city. Welcome to Crab Town. **100 pages $8**

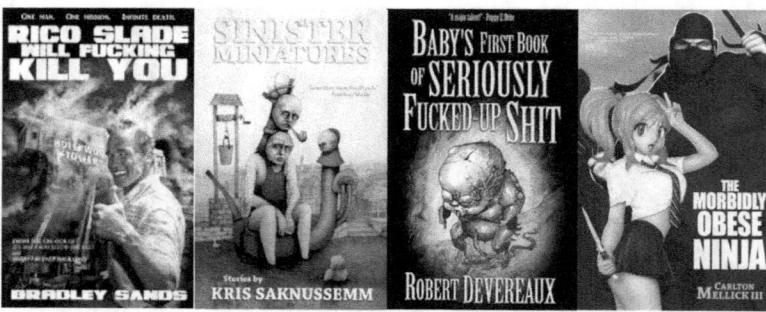

BB-119 **"Rico Slade Will Fucking Kill You" Bradley Sands** — Rico Slade is an action hero. Rico Slade can rip out a throat with his bare hands. Rico Slade's favorite food is the honey-roasted peanut. Rico Slade will fucking kill everyone. A novel. **122 pages $8**

BB-120 **"Sinister Miniatures" Kris Saknussemm** — The definitive collection of short fiction by Kris Saknussemm, confirming that he is one of the best, most daring writers of the weird to emerge in the twenty-first century. **180 pages $11**

BB-121 **"Baby's First Book of Seriously Fucked up Shit" Robert Devereaux** — Ten stories of the strange, the gross, and the just plain fucked up from one of the most original voices in horror. **176 pages $11**

BB-122 **"The Morbidly Obese Ninja" Carlton Mellick III** — These days, if you want to run a successful company . . . you're going to need a lot of ninjas. **92 pages $8**

BB-123 **"Abortion Arcade" Cameron Pierce** — An intoxicating blend of body horror and midnight movie madness, reminiscent of early David Lynch and the splatterpunks at their most sublime. **172 pages $11**

BB-124 **"Black Hole Blues" Patrick Wensink** — A hilarious double helix of country music and physics. **196 pages $11**

BB-125 **"Barbarian Beast Bitches of the Badlands" Carlton Mellick III** — Three prequels and sequels to *Warrior Wolf Women of the Wasteland*. **284 pages $13**

BB-126 **"The Traveling Dildo Salesman" Kevin L. Donihe** — A nightmare comedy about destiny, faith, and sex toys. Also featuring Donihe's most lurid and infamous short stories: *Milky Agitation, Two-Way Santa, The Helen Mower, Living Room Zombies*, and *Revenge of the Living Masturbation Rag*. **108 pages $8**

BB-127 **"Metamorphosis Blues" Bruce Taylor** — Enter a land of love beasts, intergalactic cowboys, and rock 'n roll. A land where Sears Catalogs are doorways to insanity and men keep mysterious black boxes. Welcome to the monstrous mind of Mr. Magic Realism. **136 pages $11**

BB-128 **"The Driver's Guide to Hitting Pedestrians" Andersen Prunty** — A pocket guide to the twenty-three most painful things in life, written by the most well-adjusted man in the universe. **108 pages $8**

BB-129 **"Island of the Super People" Kevin Shamel** — Four students and their anthropology professor journey to a remote island to study its indigenous population. But this is no ordinary native culture. They're super heroes and villains with flesh costumes and outlandish abilities like self-detonation, musical eyelashes, and microwave hands. **194 pages $11**

BB-130 **"Fantastic Orgy" Carlton Mellick III** — Shark Sex, mutant cats, and strange sexually transmitted diseases. Featuring the stories: *Candy-coated, Ear Cat, Fantastic Orgy, City Hobgoblins*, and *Porno in August*. **136 pages $9**

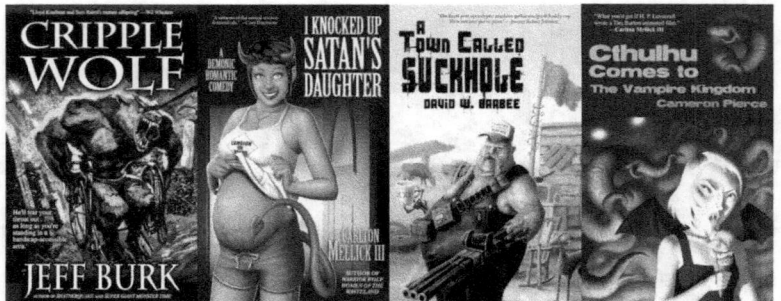

BB-131 **"Cripple Wolf" Jeff Burk** — Part man. Part wolf. 100% crippled. Also including *Punk Rock Nursing Home, Adrift with Space Badgers, Cook for Your Life, Just Another Day in the Park, Frosty and the Full Monty*, and *House of Cats*. **152 pages $10**

BB-132 **"I Knocked Up Satan's Daughter" Carlton Mellick III** — An adorable, violent, fantastical love story. A romantic comedy for the bizarro fiction reader. **152 pages $10**

BB-133 **"A Town Called Suckhole" David W. Barbee** — Far into the future, in the nuclear bowels of post-apocalyptic Dixie, there is a town. A town of derelict mobile homes, ancient junk, and mutant wildlife. A town of slack jawed rednecks who bask in the splendors of moonshine and mud boggin'. A town dedicated to the bloody and demented legacy of the Old South. A town called Suckhole. **144 pages $10**

BB-134 **"Cthulhu Comes to the Vampire Kingdom" Cameron Pierce** — What you'd get if H. P. Lovecraft wrote a Tim Burton animated film. **148 pages $11**

BB-135 **"I am Genghis Cum" Violet LeVoit** — From the savage Arctic tundra to post-partum mutations to your missing daughter's unmarked grave, join visionary madwoman Violet LeVoit in this non-stop eight-story onslaught of full-tilt Bizarro punk lit thrills. **124 pages $9**

BB-136 **"Haunt" Laura Lee Bahr** — A tripping-balls Los Angeles noir, where a mysterious dame drags you through a time-warping Bizarro hall of mirrors. **316 pages $13**

BB-137 **"Amazing Stories of the Flying Spaghetti Monster" edited by Cameron Pierce** — Like an all-spaghetti evening of Adult Swim, the Flying Spaghetti Monster will show you the many realms of His Noodly Appendage. Learn of those who worship him and the lives he touches in distant, mysterious ways. **228 pages $12**

BB-138 **"Wave of Mutilation" Douglas Lain** — A dream-pop exploration of modern architecture and the American identity, *Wave of Mutilation* is a Zen finger trap for the 21st century. **100 pages $8**

BB-139 **"Hooray for Death!" Mykle Hansen** — Famous Author Mykle Hansen draws unconventional humor from deaths tiny and large, and invites you to laugh while you can. **128 pages $10**

BB-140 **"Hypno-hog's Moonshine Monster Jamboree" Andrew Goldfarb** — Hicks, Hogs, Horror! Goldfarb is back with another strange illustrated tale of backwoods weirdness. **120 pages $9**

BB-141 **"Broken Piano For President" Patrick Wensink** — A comic masterpiece about the fast food industry, booze, and the necessity to choose happiness over work and security. **372 pages $15**

BB-142 **"Please Do Not Shoot Me in the Face" Bradley Sands** — A novel in three parts, *Please Do Not Shoot Me in the Face: A Novel*, is the story of one boy detective, the worst ninja in the world, and the great American fast food wars. It is a novel of loss, destruction, and--incredibly--genuine hope. **224 pages $12**

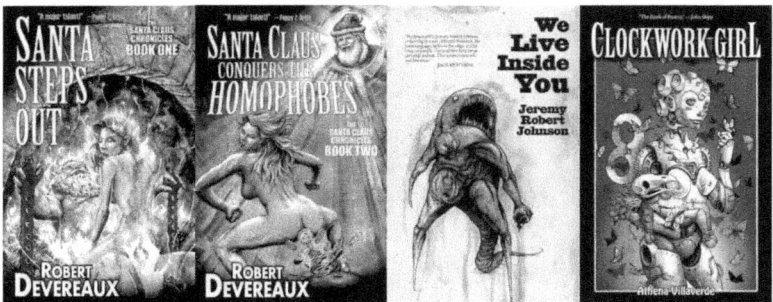

BB-143 **"Santa Steps Out" Robert Devereaux** — Sex, Death, and Santa Claus ... The ultimate erotic Christmas story is back. **294 pages $13**

BB-144 **"Santa Conquers the Homophobes" Robert Devereaux** — "I wish I could hope to ever attain one-thousandth the perversity of Robert Devereaux's toenail clippings." - Poppy Z. Brite **316 pages $13**

BB-145 **"We Live Inside You" Jeremy Robert Johnson** — "Jeremy Robert Johnson is dancing to a way different drummer. He loves language, he loves the edge, and he loves us people. These stories have range and style and wit. This is entertainment... and literature."- Jack Ketchum **188 pages $11**

BB-146 **"Clockwork Girl" Athena Villaverde** — Urban fairy tales for the weird girl in all of us. Like a combination of Francesca Lia Block, Charles de Lint, Kathe Koja, Tim Burton, and Hayao Miyazaki, her stories are cute, kinky, edgy, magical, provocative, and strange, full of poetic imagery and vicious sexuality. **160 pages $10**

BB-147 **"Armadillo Fists" Carlton Mellick III** — A weird-as-hell gangster story set in a world where people drive giant mechanical dinosaurs instead of cars. **168 pages $11**

BB-148 **"Gargoyle Girls of Spider Island" Cameron Pierce** — Four college seniors venture out into open waters for the tropical party weekend of a lifetime. Instead of a teenage sex fantasy, they find themselves in a nightmare of pirates, sharks, and sex-crazed monsters. **100 pages $8**

BB-149 **"The Handsome Squirm" by Carlton Mellick III** — Like Franz Kafka's *The Trial* meets an erotic body horror version of *The Blob*. **158 pages $11**

BB-150 **"Tentacle Death Trip" Jordan Krall** — It's *Death Race 2000* meets H. P. Lovecraft in bizarro author Jordan Krall's best and most suspenseful work to date. **224 pages $12**

BB-151 **"The Obese" Nick Antosca** — Like Alfred Hitchcock's *The Birds*... but with obese people. **108 pages $10**

BB-152 **"All-Monster Action!" Cody Goodfellow** — The world gave him a blank check and a demand: Create giant monsters to fight our wars. But Dr. Otaku was not satisfied with mere chaos and mass destruction.... **216 pages $12**

BB-153 **"Ugly Heaven" Carlton Mellick III** — Heaven is no longer a paradise. It was once a blissful utopia full of wonders far beyond human comprehension. But the afterlife is now in ruins. It has become an ugly, lonely wasteland populated by strange monstrous beasts, masturbating angels, and sad man-like beings wallowing in the remains of the once-great Kingdom of God. **106 pages $8**

BB-154 **"Space Walrus" Kevin L. Donihe** — Walter is supposed to go where no walrus has ever gone before, but all this astronaut walrus really wants is to take it easy on the intense training, escape the chimpanzee bullies, and win the love of his human trainer Dr. Stephanie. **160 pages $11**

BB-155 **"Unicorn Battle Squad" Kirsten Alene** — Mutant unicorns. A palace with a thousand human legs. The most powerful army on the planet. **192 pages $11**

BB-156 **"Kill Ball" Carlton Mellick III** — In a city where all humans live inside of plastic bubbles, exotic dancers are being murdered in the rubbery streets by a mysterious stalker known only as Kill Ball. **134 pages $10**

BB-157 **"Die You Doughnut Bastards" Cameron Pierce** — The bacon storm is rolling in. We hear the grease and sugar beat against the roof and windows. The doughnut people are attacking. We press close together, forgetting for a moment that we hate each other. **196 pages $11**

BB-158 **"Tumor Fruit" Carlton Mellick III** — Eight desperate castaways find themselves stranded on a mysterious deserted island. They are surrounded by poisonous blue plants and an ocean made of acid. Ravenous creatures lurk in the toxic jungle. The ghostly sound of crying babies can be heard on the wind. **310 pages $13**

BB-159 **"Thunderpussy" David W. Barbee** — When it comes to high-tech global espionage, only one man has the balls to save humanity from the world's most powerful bastards. He's Declan Magpie Bruce, Agent 00X. **136 pages $11**

BB-160 **"Papier Mâché Jesus" Kevin L. Donihe** — Donihe's surreal wit and beautiful mind-bending imagination is on full display with stories such as All Children Go to Hell, Happiness is a Warm Gun, and Swimming in Endless Night. **154 pages $11**

BB-161 **"Cuddly Holocaust" Carlton Mellick III** — The war between humans and toys has come to an end. The toys won. **172 pages $11**

BB-162 **"Hammer Wives" Carlton Mellick III** — Fish-eyed mutants, oceans of insects, and flesh-eating women with hammers for heads. Hammer Wives collects six of his most popular novelettes and short stories. **152 pages $10**